This b...
to Varnikha

This boo

People come from all
around Zavania to
visit the famous fairy
market, where you can buy
all sorts of beautiful things:
shimmering jewels, bright flowers,
delectable sweets! But the fairy
folk must be on guard against a
dangerous enemy, who have their
own dark magic and
mean them harm. . .

**Look out for Maddie's other
adventures in Zavania...**

Unicorn Wishes

Mermaid Wishes

Princess Wishes

Ballerina Wishes

This Book Belongs to VARNIKA

World of Wishes
Fairy Wishes

Carol Barton
Illustrated by Charlotte Alder

SCHOLASTIC

An imprint of Scholastic Ltd
Euston House, 24 Eversholt Street
London, NW1 1DB, UK

Registered office: Westfield Road, Southam, Warwickshire, CV47 0RA
SCHOLASTIC and associated logos are trademarks and or registered
trademarks of Scholastic Inc.

Text copyright © Carol Barton, 2007
Illustrations © Charlotte Alder, 2007

The right of Carol Barton to be identified as the author of this work and the
right of Charlotte Alder to be identified as the illustrator of this work
has been asserted by them.

10 digit ISBN 0 439 94363 9
13 digit ISBN 978 0439 94363 5

British Library Cataloguing-in-Publication Data
A CIP catalogue record for this book is available from the British Library
Typeset by M Rules

Paper used in this book is made from wood grown in
sustainable forests.

This is a work of fiction. Names, characters, places, incidents and dialogues are
products of the author's imagination or are used fictitiously. Any resemblance
to actual people, living or dead, events or locales is entirely coincidental.

www.scholastic.co.uk/zone

First published in the UK in 2007 by Scholastic Children's Books
Reprinted by Scholastic India Pvt. Ltd., Feb., 2008, March, 2008.

Printed at *Yash* Printographics, Noida

Contents

light

For Rebecca, with love

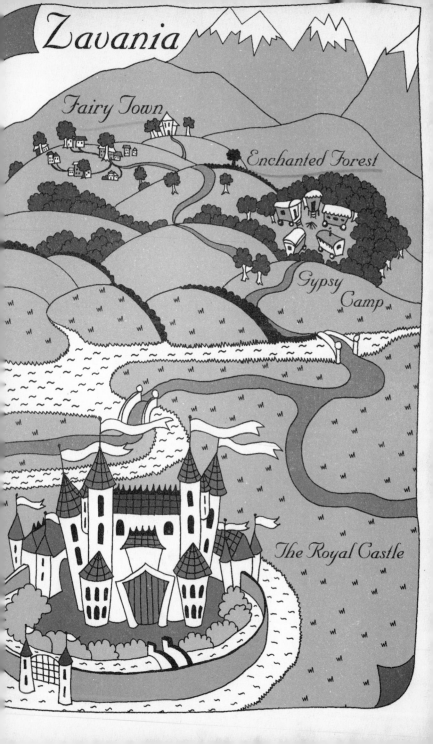

Zavania

Chapter One

The Midnight Hour

Tap, tap, tap. Tap, tap, tap.

Maddie turned over in bed, trying to ignore the noise that was threatening to wake her up. She was enjoying her dream and she knew that if she awoke the dream would be lost along with all the others that disappeared each morning, never to be repeated.

She was particularly enjoying this dream because she was back in Zavania, the

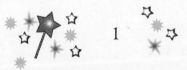

mysterious land of magic and adventure which she had visited before, the land she always lived in hope of visiting again.

She had dreamed that her friend Sebastian had come to collect her in his boat on the stream beneath the willows at the bottom of her garden. Zak the raven had been with him, just as he always was, and together they had travelled downstream to Zavania.

Tap, tap, tap. Tap, tap, tap.

There it was again. That irritating noise, just when the dream was getting to the interesting part! Just when the friends were about to discover who had made a wish. Maddie pulled her duvet up around her ears, trying to shut out the noise as she concentrated really hard on the dream.

Tap, tap, tap. Tap, tap, tap.

"Oh, for goodness' sake! What is that *noise?*" Maddie flung back her duvet and

2

leapt angrily out of bed, the dream now gone completely.

To her surprise it was still dark, very dark. She had imagined it must be morning. She hesitated for a moment, then pulled back the curtains and peered out of the window. The garden below was bathed in moonlight, but perched on the windowsill was a large black bird. As Maddie gazed in astonishment, the bird leaned forward and with its huge beak tapped on the windowpane again.

Tap, tap, tap. Tap, tap, tap.

Maddie's anger disappeared immediately and she excitedly pushed open the window. "Zak!" she cried. "Whatever are you doing here in the middle of the night?"

"Well, what do you think I'm doing here?" hissed Zak irritably. "I'm neither on a picnic, nor am I here for my health. I've come to get you, of course. I've been

3

out here for ages tapping on that window. I thought you were never going to take any notice."

"I was asleep," protested Maddie. "In fact, I was actually dreaming I was in Zavania with you and Sebastian. That's when you woke me up. . ."

"All right, all right." Zak still sounded irritable. "Now that I've succeeded in waking you, are you going to stand there nattering all night?"

"No, of course not," said Maddie. "Do you want me to come with you now?"

"Of course I do! Zenith's in a bit of a flap. He's got more work on than he can handle at the moment. Now there's this panic with his cousin, and he has to leave Zavania for a while."

"Leave Zavania?" Maddie was wide-eyed with excitement at what this might mean. Zenith was Zavania's WishMaster and in charge of wish-granting assignments. He

4

was also Sebastian's boss and always had the final word.

"Yes, that's why we need to hurry," said Zak. "We need to get back to Zavania before he goes. So get yourself dressed – wear something warm, it's a bit nippy out here. I'll wait for you in the garden and whatever you do don't make any noise; we don't want all the neighbourhood awake."

"All right," said Maddie. As she was about to close the window, she said anxiously, "Zak, about my mum. . ."

"Don't worry about her," said Zak with a sigh. "We've been through all this before. We'll have you back before she even knows you've gone."

Of course they would, she thought, as the raven flew down to the garden and she shut the window and drew her curtains once more. On the other occasions she had gone with them into Zavania, no one had had a clue that she had travelled

anywhere. Zavania was a land where time seemed to stand still and on her return little or no time seemed to have passed. But Maddie still needed that little bit of reassurance.

Quickly she changed out of her pyjamas into a pair of tracksuit trousers, a T-shirt, a warm sweater, socks and a pair of trainers. Then, very quietly, she crept out of her bedroom and down the stairs. Twice the floorboards creaked really loudly and Maddie froze, expecting her dad to appear on the landing at any moment, demanding to know where on earth she thought she was going. Nothing happened, however, and at last she let herself out of the back door and into the garden.

The night air was crisp and cold. Bathed in moonlight, the garden looked quite different from how it looked during the day. Maddie paused uncertainly on the doorstep, looking around at the silver-

6

frosted lawn, the flowerbeds and the darke
shapes of the shrubs and bushes.

And then she saw Zak. He was perched
on the bird table in the centre of the lawn.
When he caught sight of her, he flapped his
wings and Maddie knew that was the sign
for her to follow him.

The first part was easy – her trainers crunching on the frost-stiffened lawn, then down the crazy-paving pathway and under the trellis archway. Crossing the vegetable garden with its humps and stalks was a little more difficult, but somehow Maddie managed to keep up with the large black shape ahead of her until the moon disappeared behind a cloud and the garden was plunged into sudden darkness.

Maddie gasped, stumbled, then promptly walked into a tree, its damp leaves brushing her face. "Uggh!" she cried. "Oh Zak. Wait for me! Where are you? I can't see you."

But there was only silence, and no movement at all in the dense blackness ahead of her. She plunged on through the darkness, then caught a gleam of light deep in the willows right at the very bottom of the garden.

With a little sob of relief, her trainers

slipping on the soft earth, she followed the light until she reached the banks of the stream.

The boat was moored beneath the branches of the willows and the light came from a lantern that was hanging at its stern. Sebastian was there too, sitting amongst the cushions at the bottom of the boat and talking quietly to Zak, who had perched on the end of the pole while they waited for Maddie.

"Here she is," croaked Zak as Sebastian looked up. "Where've you been?" he went on. "Thought you'd gone back to bed."

"I couldn't see," protested Maddie. "The moon went in and it was pitch dark. You might have waited for me."

"That's right, you tell him," said Sebastian with a chuckle. Standing up, he grasped Maddie's outstretched hand and helped her aboard. "Hello, Maddie," he said.

9

"Hello, Sebastian," she replied, and she felt all warm inside like she always did when she stepped aboard Sebastian's boat.

"Sorry about the rush," he said.

"That's OK," Maddie replied, a little gruffly. She didn't really care what time of the day or night it was, just as long as they came to get her and she could go with them. "Zak says there's a bit of a panic on."

"Well, I wouldn't exactly say *panic*." Sebastian glared at Zak as he took the pole and began to push the boat away from the bank. "It's just that Zenith is really busy and we need to get to the East Tower before he leaves to visit his cousin."

"Who is his cousin?" asked Maddie curiously. She sank down among the cushions and took the rug that Sebastian handed to her, tucking it cosily around her legs and feet. Zak had been quite right when he had said it was cold.

"His name is Suleiman," Sebastian replied.

"So is he a WishMaster like Zenith?" asked Maddie.

"No," Sebastian answered, "Suleiman is a genie. He lives in a far-off desert land. He's sent for Zenith to help him – it appears he's got himself into a bit of a state."

"Why don't you just get to the point?" said Zak with a wicked cackle. "Basically, he's been stuffing himself on so much sherbet and Turkish Delight and put on so much weight that he can't get into his magic lamp."

"Zak. . ." began Sebastian warningly.

"Well, it's true." Zak tossed his head. "And let's face it, a genie that can't get into his lamp is no use to anyone."

"No," agreed Maddie, "I don't suppose he is. So if Zenith has to go away to the desert, what do we have to do?"

"Good question," snorted Zak. "We have to take over Zenith's latest

11

assignment. Another wish has been made but Zenith was so angry about Suleiman I've been keeping out of his way. Last time I got in his way when he was in one of his moods he threatened to have Thirza make me into a raven pie."

"Who has made a wish this time?" asked Maddie.

"It was brought to Zavania through a messenger," said Sebastian," wasn't it, Zak?"

"Yep." Zak hunched his wings, perched on the top of the lantern as they glided through the inky blackness of the water. "Zenith told us to come and get you, Maddie, and to hurry straight back."

"Did he really?" Maddie flushed with pleasure and was glad of the cover of darkness. "Perhaps he thinks you'll need help writing the spells, Sebastian."

"And learning 'em," chuckled Zak. "You'd think he'd know how to do them by

12

now, wouldn't you? I dread to think where we'd be without you, Maddie."

"Well, you won't be without me because I'm here now," said Maddie stoutly.

"Thank you, Maddie," said Sebastian, throwing her a grateful glance.

"Anyway, I like writing poetry and verses and things," she said. "But you haven't told me whose wish it is – and who was this messenger who brought it to Zavania?"

"His name is Reuben," Sebastian replied. "He is a tinker who travels regularly to Zavania and other areas, selling his wares."

"And the wish?" breathed Maddie.

"Made by one of the fairy folk, apparently."

Maddie looked sharply at Sebastian to see if he was joking but he appeared to be quite serious. "A fairy?" she repeated almost in disbelief.

Sebastian nodded.

"But. . . but I didn't think there was any such things as fairies," protested Maddie.

"Oh boy!" squawked Zak and flapped his wings.

"Oh, Maddie, Maddie," said Sebastian softly.

Maddie frowned. "Well, I used to believe in them when I was younger, but now . . . well. . ." She trailed off uncertainly.

"And how many times have you come to Zavania?" demanded Zak, turning round several times on his perch.

"Four times. . ." Maddie began uncertainly.

"Then you should know by now that in Zavania nothing is impossible," snorted Zak.

"Yes, right," said Maddie in a small voice. "I'm sorry." She took a deep breath. "So a fairy has made a wish – do we know what this wish is?"

"Oh yes," Sebastian replied. "The fairy

14

told Reuben that she wished they could be free again."

"Free from what?" Maddie asked.

"That," said Sebastian firmly, "is what we have to find out."

Chapter Two

Inside the Turret Room

Maddie snuggled down under the rug, nestling even deeper into the softness of the cushions. This journey into Zavania was completely different to the others she had made. Those had been in daytime, when the mist had swirled around the boat and then drifted away to reveal bright sunlight dancing on the water, days when the fields on either side had been packed with flowers – the scarlet of poppies, yellow

cowslips, daisies and the bright blue of cornflowers.

Now all was darkness, with black shapes looming on either side – whether trees, bushes or rocks it was impossible to say – as the boat sped on to the land of magic. Maddie would have been scared by the eerie darkness and the silence had she been alone, but with Sebastian behind her and Zak up ahead she had no fears.

Because it was the middle of the night when they finally slipped into the stream in the gardens of the royal castle and moored the boat beside the jetty, there was none of the splendour and colour of previous occasions. But in spite of the fact that Maddie couldn't see the flags and pennants that flew from the battlements or the mass of flowers in the gardens or the fountains with their raspberry-flavoured water, there was somehow an even greater sense of excitement as, like shadows in the night,

17

she and Sebastian flitted through the gardens with Zak flying alongside.

Apart from the odd torch that flamed here and there on the battlements, the bulk of the castle was in darkness while its inhabitants slept, but as the friends rounded the corner at the end of the gardens it was to find that the East Tower was a blaze of lights.

"What's going on here?" muttered Zak.

"I don't know," said Sebastian. "We'd better go and find out."

Inside the tower they found Thirza, the WishMaster's tiny housekeeper, running to and fro packing things into a large, soft, tapestry bag with leather handles. When she caught sight of the friends she stopped and threw up her hands. "Well, at last," she cried in her shrill, bell-like voice. "I thought you weren't going to get here in time. He's in a right old state, I can tell you." She rolled her eyes heavenwards –

18

and the friends knew there was no doubt as to whom she was referring.

"In time for what?" asked Sebastian urgently. "What is it, Thirza? What's happening?"

"He had another message from Suleiman – it seems because he can't get into his lamp and perform his magic the Sultan may expel him from the palace. Anyway, poor old Suleiman is in absolute terror now and has begged Zenith to go there straight away."

"But he hasn't given me any instructions about the assignment yet." Sebastian went pale.

"That's why he wants to see you before he goes," Thirza said firmly. "He said to go straight up the minute you arrive – but that was ages ago."

"I can just imagine the mood he must be in," muttered Zak. "If it's all the same to you, old son, I think I'll stay down here

while you go up and see him." With that, the raven promptly put his head under his wing.

"Oh no you don't," said Sebastian swiftly. "You can't get out of it that easily. You'll come up with us. And you needn't think you can get out of it by pretending to be asleep," he added as there came a loud snore from under Zak's wing.

"You all have to go," said Thirza, putting pay to any further argument. "That was Zenith's orders, so go on, up you go."

And if there was any further doubt, at that very moment the door at the top of the stairs was flung back on its hinges and there came a huge roar of anger. "What are you chattering about, you miserable wretches? Have you no sense of time? Do you not realize I could have you all turned into frogs for keeping me waiting?"

The friends froze and stared up at the terrifying figure of the WishMaster, who

towered above them with his arms folded and legs apart. His black cloak billowed around him and his bald head shone in the light from a torch that flared in a bracket on the stone wall. The fearsome black eyebrows that Maddie remembered so well seemed to bristle more than ever.

"We . . . we're so . . . sorry . . . we're . . . late," stammered Sebastian, as he desperately tried to draw himself up and take control, as befitted his role as Junior WishMaster.

"Yes, we got here as soon as we could. . ." Even Zak attempted to placate their Master.

"Silence, miserable bird," thundered Zenith, and Zak shrank back with a squawk and a twitter. "Any more from you and you'll end up as the stuffing in one of Thirza's cushions."

The sheer awfulness of this prospect seemed to ensure silence from the raven at

least for the moment, and even Sebastian seemed awed into a dumbstruck trance. In the end it was Maddie who stepped forward and ran up the steps, as light as thistledown, her red curls bobbing.

"Hello, Zenith," she said cheerfully, even though inside she was quaking. "You mustn't blame Sebastian or Zak for being late. It was my fault, you see. I was asleep and I couldn't wake up. But we're all here now." As she reached the top step beside the WishMaster, Maddie brushed past and danced away into the turret room.

There was a stunned silence behind her. Then a bemused Zenith came into the turret room, followed a few seconds later by an equally shocked Sebastian and Zak.

"So what is it you want us to do this time?" asked Maddie calmly. "I understand you have to go and help your poor cousin?"

"Yes." Zenith still seemed somewhat bewildered as he stood in the centre of the

22

room with its shelves full of pills and potions and strange-looking instruments. He gazed uncertainly at each of the friends. "In fact, I have to leave immediately for the desert lands. You know another wish has been made?" He frowned at Maddie.

"Yes," she said. "A fairy, I believe?"

Zenith nodded. "I decided this was to be an Official Wish and that I would grant it, but because of these new circumstances Sebastian will have to take over." He sounded as if he doubted the friends would cope.

"Oh, I'm sure it will be all right," said Maddie, clasping her hands together.

"Huruump!" said Zenith, as if he still wasn't entirely convinced.

"What instructions do you have for me?" asked Sebastian nervously.

"You know the form," said Zenith sternly. "At least you should by now – not that you've yet had anything too taxing to

 23

grant. As you know, the fairy has wished that they – presumably the fairy folk – could be free again. We don't, however, know what it is she wishes them to be free from. You will need to talk to Reuben, the tinker who brought the wish to us. You will write yourself two spells as usual and make the choice of ring as your conductor of magic."

"Are you imposing any restrictions?" asked Sebastian.

"Only one," replied Zenith.

"Wait for it," muttered Zak to Maddie.

"What did you say?" demanded Zenith, rounding on the raven.

"Nothing!" squawked Zak. "Nothing at all."

"My only restriction is that your spells should be made up with the letter Q," said Zenith, still staring suspiciously at the raven.

Sebastian gave a little groan of despair

24

but Maddie simply tossed her head. "That's all right, Sebastian," she said, "it won't be a problem."

Sebastian looked far from convinced but Zenith obviously didn't intend hanging around any longer. "I can't stand here talking all night," he said impatiently, "I need to be on my way."

"Is there nothing else you need to tell us?" There was a definite note of panic in Sebastian's voice as it finally sank in that his Master was once again leaving him in charge of granting an Official Wish.

"You will do as you have always done," said Zenith, and Maddie thought he sounded a little more kindly now. "You will make the spells wisely, using your judgement and skill. There is, however, one word of warning I will leave you with."

"What is that?" said Sebastian, his voice barely more than a whisper.

"We know little of the nature of this

wish, therefore we know little of any danger it might bring. I myself have spoken to the tinker and what he has told me leaves me with no choice but to tell you to proceed with extreme caution."

With that warning ringing in their ears, Zenith led the way down the stairs. Leaving the friends on the steps outside the East Tower, he started out in his horse-drawn carriage on the first stage of his long journey to the desert lands.

"Well, I suppose we'd better get on with it," said Sebastian as the sound of the horses' hooves died away and they all turned and trailed back inside.

"Not before you have something to eat and drink some of my strawberry cordial," said Thirza firmly. "You'll feel much better after that and more able to work."

And she was right. The food and cordial seemed to revive their spirits and when they had finished they once more made their way up into the turret room.

"What shall we do first?" whispered Maddie, looking around her at the dozens of bottles full of different coloured potions and the shelves stacked with dusty books.

"We will choose the ring as our conductor of magic," Sebastian replied in the same rather hushed tones. For the first time, Maddie noticed that he wore a large bunch of keys on a chain around his waist. Selecting one of the keys, and watched by

Maddie and Zak, he crossed the turret room, unlocked a large display case and lifted back the lid. Maddie followed him cautiously and the sight that met her eyes took her breath away. On a bed of black velvet were three rows of rings, their precious stones twinkling in the light from the flaming torches around the walls.

"Oh!" she gasped. "I'd forgotten how beautiful they are! Look, Sebastian." She pointed to one of the rings. "There's the emerald we used for the unicorn's wish."

"And there's the topaz we used for the princess's wish," cackled Zak. Then, as if he'd just thought of it, he said in sudden alarm, "she's not coming with us this time, is she, Sebastian?"

Sebastian shook his head and, like Zak, Maddie breathed a sigh of relief. "As far as I know she doesn't know anything about this wish and I think I'd like to keep it that way."

"Too right, old son," muttered Zak. "More trouble than she's worth, that one. Now, let's see, which ring has our master taken off with him to the desert?"

"The ruby," said Sebastian.

"Well, that figures! Just about the most potent stone there is, and he snaffles it."

"He *is* the boss," protested Sebastian mildly, "and he will probably need it. I gather the desert can be a very dangerous place."

"Well, the land of the fairies might be even *more* dangerous," sniffed Zak, but the idea seemed so silly that they all ended up laughing.

"So which ring do you think we should use?" asked Maddie.

"Since we used that diamond for the ballerina's wish, how about that rather handsome sapphire?" said Zak, pointing with his wing.

"Which one do you think, Maddie?"

asked Sebastian. "Which stone do you think would be suitable to help grant the fairy's wish?"

"I think. . ." said Maddie, "that one there would be just right." She pointed at a lovely soft purple one. "It reminds me of how I imagine fairies' wings."

"The amethyst," said Sebastian. "A very good choice – the amethyst it shall be. But now we have the difficult part, because we have to write the spells."

"I told you, Sebastian, you needn't worry about that," said Maddie lightly. "It's the letter Q, isn't it?"

"Yes," Sebastian replied gloomily, "and I can't think of anything."

"Oh boy," said Zak, "we could be here for hours. I'm going to get some shut-eye."

"Come on," said Maddie. "Let's start looking up words beginning with Q in Zenith's books. Honestly, Sebastian, it won't take long – I promise."

Chapter Three

Reuben the Tinker

"So have you finished then?" Zak had been snoozing on his perch while Sebastian and Maddie worked on the spells, but on hearing sounds of movement from the end of the room he poked his beak out from under his wing.

"Yes, we have," said Sebastian, and the relief in his voice was only too obvious. "Thanks to Maddie. I really don't know what I'd do without her."

"Quite," cackled Zak. "It would have been like the time you wrote a spell and it didn't work because the verse didn't rhyme – pretty embarrassing that, wasn't it, old son?"

Sebastian shuddered. "Don't remind me. I thought Zenith was going to take my Golden Spurs back."

"Well, let's hear them," said Zak.

"Actually," said Sebastian, "I think we should go and talk to Reuben the Tinker now."

"OK." Zak stretched and flapped his wings a couple of times. "Just as long as you remember that it's forbidden to take written spells away from here – you have to memorize them. That's one of Zenith's strictest rules."

"That's no problem," said Maddie, tossing back her hair. "We know them already, don't we, Sebastian?"

"I bet *he* doesn't," said Zak with a sly chuckle.

"Well, I do," said Maddie, "so if Sebastian forgets anything I can remind him."

Together they left the East Tower and made their way across to the royal castle. It was daylight now, and early morning sunshine bathed the castle and the gardens in a soft golden glow, but to Maddie's surprise she didn't feel the tiniest bit tired. They passed the sentries who challenged them just as they always did, pretending they didn't know who they were, and into the royal mews.

"Reuben stays in one of the rooms above the stalls when he visits Zavania," Sebastian explained to Maddie as they walked under a stone archway and into the stable yard.

"Is he nice?" asked Maddie, gazing at the horses who looked out at them over the doors of their stalls and whickered gently as they passed.

33

"He's OK," said Sebastian slowly, "but . . . he's a bit . . . a bit odd in some ways."

"You can say that again," said Zak with a sniff. "And as for that pet of his, well, someone should put it in a bucket of water—"

"Zak," said Sebastian warningly.

"So what exactly is this pet?" asked Maddie. "And what has it done?"

"It's a magpie," Sebastian explained, "its name is Mishka . . . and—"

"Nasty, vicious, brute," Zak interrupted. "I don't like him, never have."

"And he probably doesn't like you either," said Sebastian.

"Eh? What?" Zak looked astonished that anyone might not like him.

"Reuben is obviously very fond of him," Sebastian went on. "So much so that Mishka goes everywhere with him, riding on his shoulder."

 34

"Still don't like him," muttered Zak under his breath. "I say," he said in sudden alarm, "they won't be coming with us on this assignment, will they?"

"I've no idea," Sebastian replied. "In fact, I really know very little about the whole thing. Now, let me see . . ." He looked up above one of the stables. "Yes, this is the one. Come on, follow me."

They trooped into the stables, then stopped as someone shouted out from the top of a flight of wooden steps that led to a hayloft.

"Reuben, is that you?" called Sebastian. "Can we come up?"

"Yes, come up," called the voice, and Maddie and Zak followed Sebastian up the steps. It was rather dim in the loft above the stables, the only light coming from shafts of sunlight that filtered through the slats of the shutters. As Maddie's gaze became accustomed to the

gloom, she saw a bedroll was stacked neatly in one corner and there, in the middle of the room, the man who called himself Reuben the Tinker. He was tall and very thin with a long nose and rather sad eyes. He wore a high velvet hat with a long feather tucked into the band, a multi-coloured waistcoat, breeches and soft leather boots that reached his knees. On his shoulder sat Mishka the magpie, who watched them all with a suspicious stare.

"Hello, Reuben," said Sebastian, shaking hands with the tinker. "Zenith has been unexpectedly called away and he's asked me to take over the granting of the fairy's wish."

"I see," said Reuben uncertainly, his gaze flickering to Maddie.

"This is Maddie," said Sebastian, "who will be helping us in this assignment. Maddie, this is Reuben."

36

"Hello, Reuben," said Maddie shyly.

"Have I seen you before?" The tinker's eyes narrowed.

It was Sebastian who answered. "Maddie is from the Other Place," he explained.

"Is that wise?" The tinker raised one eyebrow and his magpie gave a loud squawk, which caused Zak to begin pacing up and down the loft floor in agitation. "Whenever I've had any dealings with anyone from the Other Place it's always ended in disaster."

"Oh, that won't happen with Maddie," said Sebastian quickly. "She's helped us several times before and it was Zenith himself who suggested she might help with this particular wish."

This seemed to reassure the tinker, but the magpie still seemed wary and Zak continued his pacing.

"Reuben, will you tell us everything

37

you can about the wish?" Sebastian paused and looked over his shoulder. "Zak," he said sternly, "will you please stop pacing up and down and go perch somewhere."

The magpie cackled with glee at his words while Zak stopped in his tracks, disgruntled at being told off in front of them all. With a toss of his head, he flew up on to a beam where he sat in a huff with his back to them.

"Why don't you sit down?" Reuben indicated bales of straw and waited while Sebastian and Maddie made themselves comfortable. Then, choosing to stand himself, he set about explaining the details of the wish. "My home," he said, "is in the north-east. I often tour Zavania selling my wares and occasionally my travels take me through the glens and dells of the fairy folk. I have to say they've always made me very welcome. They are

lovely, gentle folk, always ready to do a kindness to weary travellers – which is why what happened this time seems so strange."

"So what did happen?" Maddie's eyes widened and she leaned forward so as not to miss anything the tinker might have to say.

"From the moment I arrived in their land I felt something was wrong," said Reuben. "Even Mishka thought so, didn't you, my beauty?" He turned his head towards the magpie on his shoulder, who twittered softly in agreement.

"What sort of wrong?" asked Sebastian with a frown.

"It was difficult to pinpoint anything exactly – it was several little things. For example, no one offered us anywhere to stay for the night."

"And do they usually?" asked Maddie.

"Oh yes," Reuben replied, "every time.

The fairy folk are second to none when it comes to hospitality and as for their market, well, people come from miles around to buy their beautiful goods. They usually invite me to set up my stall in the market and sell my wares but this time no one came forward even to speak to me."

"Was there any sign of Tatiana?" asked Sebastian.

"Who's Tatiana?" asked Maddie, her eyes like saucers at all this talk of real fairies.

"Don't you know *anything*?" hissed the magpie. "I thought you were supposed to be useful!"

"Oi!" Zak spun round on his perch and glared indignantly at the magpie. "Don't speak to Maddie like that. She asked a simple question and she deserves a simple answer."

"Well, for goodness' sake!" Mishka hunched his head down between his wings.

"Everyone knows who Tatiana is."

"Tatiana is the queen of the fairies, Maddie," Sebastian explained kindly. Turning to Reuben again, and ignoring the warring birds, he asked, "Is she usually around when you visit the fairy dells?"

"I usually catch a glimpse of her somewhere," Reuben replied, "perhaps flying to visit someone who is sick, but even if I don't actually see her there is usually a lot of talk about her."

"And this time?" breathed Maddie.

"This time, nothing," Reuben replied. "No glimpses, no talk, nothing."

There was a long silence in the hayloft as the friends considered what the tinker had said. In the end it was Sebastian who broke that silence. "So was there anything else?" he asked at last.

"Nothing I could really put my finger on . . . but. . ." Reuben hesitated.

"Yes. . . ?" prompted Maddie.

"There was just this feeling that something was not right. In fact, if I'm really honest, something was very, very wrong. The fairy folk seemed frightened of something but I don't know what. They seemed to be looking over their shoulders all the time, avoiding eye contact, that sort of thing."

"And the wish?" asked Maddie. "What happened about the wish?"

"Ah yes, the wish," said Reuben. "Well, that happened just as I was leaving. I'd packed all my goods into my cart and Noah, Miska and myself were trundling down through the main street of the town. . ."

"Noah?" said Maddie.

"His horse, of course!" squawked Mishka, ignoring Zak's scowl.

"The main dell was deserted," Reuben went on, "with not a soul in sight, but I

had the feeling we were being watched. Anyway, we'd reached the very end of the dell and Noah stopped to drink from the trough when quite suddenly a young fairy appeared from under the water pump. I quickly realized that she knew she would be hidden by the pump from anyone in the dell."

"Did you recognize her?" asked Sebastian.

"Yes." Reuben nodded. "Her name is Isabella. She's actually a Tooth Fairy."

"What!" exclaimed Maddie, but fell silent as Mishka turned his head and glared at her.

"She asked me if I was going to Zavania and when I said that I was, she asked if I would take a wish to Zenith the WishMaster. I said of course I would," Reuben went on, "if that was what she wanted, and then I asked her what the wish was. She seemed very frightened

 44

and spoke fast – she said that her wish was that they could be free again. I tried to ask her what it was she wanted to be free from but she looked terrified and said that she'd said enough and that she had to go."

"So you don't have any idea what she was talking about?" asked Sebastian.

"No, I don't," Reuben replied. "Not really." He hesitated. "I only know something was very wrong there, that the fairy folk weren't themselves and that they seemed frightened of something, or someone."

"So if we are to grant Isabella's wish, then it's our job to find out what the problem is," said Sebastian grimly. "Tell me, Reuben, are you intending to go back through the fairy kingdom on your way home?"

"I could go that way," Reuben replied, but he sounded doubtful – almost as if he

didn't really want to. Perhaps he too was afraid of whatever it was that was terrifying the fairy folk.

"I'd be grateful if you would," said Sebastian. "Then we could travel with you."

Zak gave a muffled snort.

"Very well, if it would help," said Reuben at last, with a sigh. "But you do know that means travelling through the Enchanted Forest, don't you?"

"Oh no," whispered Maddie. "I don't like the Enchanted Forest."

"It'll be all right, Maddie," said Sebastian soothingly, "trust me."

"Wait a moment." It was the magpie who suddenly spoke, startling everyone with its shrill voice. "Is that crow coming with us?"

"What!" spluttered Zak, looking up sharply. "Crow? *Crow?* I'm not a crow. I'll have you know I'm a raven. And not just

any old raven either, but a raven with royal connections."

"Is he coming?" demanded Mishka, ignoring Zak's ramblings.

"Well. . ." Reuben glanced at Sebastian. "Does he *have* to come?"

"Yes," Sebastian replied quietly, "just as the magpie travels with you, the raven goes with me."

"Then it shall be so." The tinker shrugged his shoulders, then raised a warning finger to the magpie, who was twittering loudly. "If it's all the same to you, I had intended leaving Zavania this morning."

"That's fine by us," Sebastian replied. "Isn't it?" He glanced at the others.

"Of course," said Maddie.

"Zak?" said Sebastian sharply when the raven didn't reply. "Are you happy with that?"

"Deliriously," muttered Zak. "A journey

through the perils of the Enchanted Forest, into unknown dangers where heaven only knows what awaits us, and all in the company of a pesky magpie. I can't wait."

Chapter Four

Into the Enchanted Forest

They left the royal mews almost immediately, travelling in Reuben's brightly painted wagon, now almost empty of his wares, and drawn by Noah, his horse.

Maddie and Sebastian rode alongside Reuben at the front of the wagon, with Mishka perched upon Reuben's shoulder, while Zak chose to fly alongside. Sometimes he paused to rest on the roof of the wagon – much to the irritation of

Mishka, who chattered angrily whenever it happened.

It was still early morning and as they left the castle its inhabitants were only just awake and setting about their daily routine.

"So what do you do in the Other Place?" Reuben asked Maddie with a sideways glance in her direction as they bumped over the cobbles outside the castle.

"I live with my mum and dad," she replied. "Oh, and Whisker, my cat," she added as an afterthought. Mention of a cat brought forth a frenzied response from the magpie, who began chattering and squawking.

"It's all right, Mishka, my beauty," soothed Reuben, "the cat is not here." He paused and looked at Maddie again. "At least I don't think he is. You don't have him with you, do you?"

"Oh no," said Maddie, "he's at home."

"Big ginger thing he is," chortled Zak. "I've seen him – he'd make mincemeat of you," he added slyly to the magpie, who responded with another torrent of squawking.

"Zak," said Sebastian warningly.

"OK!" Zak shrugged. "I'm just saying, that's all."

"What else do you do in the Other Place?" asked Reuben after a moment.

"I go to school," Maddie replied.

"Do you like school?" The tinker seemed really interested.

"Sometimes." Maddie wrinkled her nose. "I like some of the lessons, like drama and poetry, and I have a best friend, Lucy, but there are some things I don't like at all."

"What sort of things?" Reuben frowned.

"I don't like it when I'm teased," said Maddie quietly.

51

"What do you get teased about?"

"The colour of my hair, my freckles, and this dreadful brace I have to wear on my teeth."

"And who is it who teases you about these things?" asked the tinker. By this time they had left the castle behind and were bumping and jolting down a lane with steep banks on either side.

"A girl called Jessica Coatsworth," Maddie replied miserably.

"Well, I can't think why," said Reuben. "You look fine to me."

"I always feel better in Zavania," said Maddie, cheering up.

They travelled on in silence for some considerable way, the only sounds the steady clip-clop of Noah's hooves and the trundling of the wagon wheels. Finally, Reuben spoke. "We are approaching the edge of the Enchanted Forest!"

Maddie gave a shiver of fear as the

dense, dark mass of the forest loomed up ahead of them and she huddled a little closer to Sebastian.

She'd been in the Enchanted Forest before and hadn't liked it at all; she couldn't really see that it was going to be any different on this occasion.

It seemed in no time at all they had entered the forest and it grew dark and decidedly colder as the sun was blotted out by the denseness of the trees. Even Zak stayed close, and instead of flying alongside took to perching on Noah's halter – causing great agitation to the magpie.

"Leave him be," said Reuben to his pet, "he's doing no harm." The magpie was quiet after that, just giving the occasional muffled squawk to remind Zak of his presence.

As they travelled deeper into the forest the pathway grew narrower and narrower, the trees and bushes appearing to crowd in on either side.

53

54

"I really don't like it in here," said Maddie at last. "I can't see why it's called the Enchanted Forest – it should be the Scary Forest. I've always hated the place."

"When were you here before?" asked Reuben curiously.

"It was when we were returning Peregrine the unicorn to his herd," explained Maddie. "And we also travelled through it when we were looking for Princess Lyra's brother. It was scariest when we were with Peregrine, though."

"But what you have to remember," said Sebastian, "is that at that time we had the Ice Queen to deal with and her army of Ice Soldiers – they aren't here now, Maddie."

"Thanks to your spells," said Maddie.

"Sounds like these spells of yours are pretty potent," remarked Reuben.

"We may not have the Ice Queen to deal with," said Sebastian, "but what we have to remember is that no matter what

55

danger we face, we have magic to see us through."

"I wish we could use one of the spells to get us through this forest quickly," muttered Maddie with a shiver.

"Oh Maddie, you know we can't do that," said Sebastian, putting one arm around her. "We must save the spells for when we face real problems, and scary as it might be in here I can't see that we are in any real danger."

"I know," said Maddie, "but I still don't like it. I'm sure those trees have faces! I'm just glad I'm up here on the wagon and not walking – last time we were here the roots and branches kept grabbing me."

"People forget that trees are living things," said Reuben calmly. "Why shouldn't they have faces?"

"I'm not going to look," said Maddie, and hid her face in Sebastian's cloak.

"How long do you think it will take us

56

to get through the forest?" asked Sebastian.

"We should be through by tomorrow morning," Reuben replied.

"Tomorrow morning!" cried Maddie. "Do you mean we have to spend the night in this awful place?"

"It might not be as bad as you think," Reuben replied.

"Why, what are you suggesting?" asked Sebastian.

"I didn't want to say anything until I was sure," Reuben replied, "but I think I know of somewhere we can spend the night. Mishka, my beauty," he said, turning his head to look at the magpie on his shoulder, "you know what I mean. I want you to fly on ahead and find Joel."

"Why me?" The magpie tossed his head. "Why can't that crow go?"

"Watch it. . ." muttered Zak threateningly.

"I want you to go," said Reuben, "because Zak doesn't know the way."

"So with a bit of luck he'd get well and truly lost," hissed Mishka.

"Mishka!" said Reuben sternly.

"Who's Joel?" asked Maddie curiously as the magpie made a great performance of taking off.

"You'll have to wait and see," Reuben replied. "I don't want to say too much in case Mishka can't find him."

Chapter Five

The Encampment

They travelled on for a while and just when Maddie was beginning to think their progress through the forest would never end, there was a sudden whirling and swishing sound and the magpie appeared, circling once and coming to rest on Reuben's shoulder.

"Oh, here we go," muttered Zak. "Wait for it. . ."

59

"What did you find, my beauty?" murmured Reuben.

"They're there," said the magpie, keeping a wary eye on Zak, "up ahead in their usual clearing. I spoke to Joel and told him we were coming and he said they would prepare for us and that we are welcome to join them and spend the night with them."

"They know we have company?" said Reuben.

"Yes, I said there were two extra," Mishka replied.

"Er, hang on," said Zak. "What about me?"

"What about you?" said the magpie haughtily.

"Well, didn't you tell them – whoever *they* are – that I'm here too?"

"Why should I do that?" The magpie sniffed disdainfully.

"It'll be all right, Zak," Reuben said

soothingly. "You'll be welcome as well – you'll see."

Far from convinced, Zak turned his back and went into the deepest of sulks while the magpie twittered and preened itself, proud of its achievement in securing shelter for everyone for the night.

They travelled on for some considerable distance, then suddenly Maddie sat up straighter and peered ahead into the gloom. "Look," she said at last, "what's that glow over there?"

Sebastian followed her gaze. Sure enough, far ahead in the darkness of the forest a faint glow could be seen. "I don't know," he said. "Do you know, Reuben? Is this where we are heading?"

"It is," Reuben replied calmly. "Nearly there now."

"But where is there?" said Maddie impatiently. "Where are we going?"

"Wait and see," Reuben replied maddeningly.

The glow grew brighter and stronger as they travelled towards it, until at last the pathway that they had followed for so long suddenly opened up into a huge clearing and Maddie saw that the light came partly from a campfire and partly from several lanterns hanging on the branches of the trees surrounding the clearing. Beneath the lanterns were at least a dozen caravans, their dark woodwork painted with brightly coloured flowers and birds. The horses were tethered alongside, quietly grazing.

The many folk from the caravans were dotted around, some busy tending the fire or cooking in a large black pot, others sitting on the steps of their caravans engaged in woodcarving or other crafts, while yet more stood in little groups talking, laughing or arguing. There was a smell of woodsmoke, and from the

campfire a thin column of smoke drifted to the sky.

"Oh!" gasped Maddie. "It's a gypsy camp!"

"Well, bless my soul!" cried Zak. "I never did. Where have this lot come from, Reuben?"

"They originally came from a land to

the east," Reuben explained, "but for many years they've simply travelled from one place to another. They make things out of wood and leather and they exchange what they make for food."

"Are they friendly?" asked Zak dubiously. "One or two of them look a bit surly. Uh-oh, they've seen us, one of them is coming over now. . ."

One of the gypsy men, a thickset fellow with black hair and wearing a red shirt and rough homespun trousers, was indeed moving across the clearing towards them.

"They are very friendly," Reuben said softly, "though wary at first. If they make friends with you, you will be their friend for life."

"What if they *don't* make friends, that's what I'm worried about," muttered Zak, but there was no further time for idle chat since the man had reached them. Maddie noticed that he wore gold hoops in his ears

and a red and white spotted neckerchief.

By this time Reuben had jumped down from the wagon and the other two followed suit.

"Reuben, my friend! Greetings!" The man clasped Reuben in a bear hug. "You are welcome as always. As are these, your companions." His dark gaze flickered to Sebastian and Maddie.

"Joel, it's good to see you again!" Reuben stepped back and smiled, but Maddie suspected the bear hug had taken his breath away. "Yes, this is Sebastian, who is a Junior WishMaster, and his friend Maddie, who is from the Other Place . . . but don't worry," he added hastily when he saw Joel's brow darken, "she's OK. Oh yes, and this is Zak, the raven."

"You are welcome, all of you," said Joel, "and what we have is yours. Come and rest awhile and later you will share our supper." As they began to follow him into the

centre of the clearing, Joel threw Sebastian a sidelong glance. "A Junior WishMaster you say? Who do you work for?"

"Zenith the WishMaster," Sebastian replied and Maddie could not fail to hear the pride in his voice.

"I met Zenith once," Joel replied, "a fine man." He paused. "So are you on a mission?"

"Yes, we are," Sebastian replied. "Reuben has brought a wish to us – which we are on an assignment to grant."

"Good for you," said Joel. "Now, come and meet my wife, Juliana."

Joel's wife was seated on the steps of their caravan, engaged in tying sweet-smelling lavender into bunches. She looked up as they approached and Maddie found herself looking into a pair of the darkest eyes she had ever seen. More greetings followed.

"Are the girls back yet?" asked Joel,

looking beyond his wife into the caravan.

"No, not yet," Juliana replied and just for one moment Maddie thought she detected a trace of anxiety in her voice.

"They'll be home soon," Joel said. Turning to Maddie and Sebastian, he explained, "My daughters Luisa and Gabrielle have gone to the fairy market in the dell, you'll meet them on their return. But in the meantime, please make yourselves at home."

"Should we tell them," asked Maddie anxiously as they moved away from Joel's caravan, "about the fairy's wish and the strange things that are going on in the land of the fairies?"

"Best not," said Reuben. "It'll only worry them. Let's wait until after the girls come home."

The friends were quickly drawn into the warm and rather exciting atmosphere of

the gypsy encampment. They met other members of the group and were invited to sit around the fire, where they were given tin plates bearing generous helpings of the delicious-smelling stew together with dumplings, vegetables and large chunks of bread. Even Zak and Mishka appeared to have forgotten their differences as they pecked up the titbits that were provided for them by the gypsies.

After they had finished eating and the plates were cleared away someone began playing a mouth organ and when Maddie turned to see she was surprised to find that it was Reuben. Others with violins and tambourine quickly joined him and two of the gypsy girls began dancing, their skirts swirling, the coins around their foreheads glinting and their dark eyes flashing in the firelight.

"It's wonderful," cried Maddie as she clasped her hands together, caught up in

the excitement and the beat of the music.

The music grew fast and furious and seemed to go on for ever; the dancers whirled faster and faster until quite suddenly the music stopped and, amidst applause, dancers and musicians went in search of refreshment.

At that moment there was a sudden commotion on the edge of the encampment and two girls burst through the circle of caravans.

"Hello," said Zak cocking his head, "what's going on here?"

"Those are Joel's girls," murmured Reuben. "Looks as if they are in a bit of a state. Let's go and see what's happened."

Together with Reuben and Mishka, the friends made their way across to Joel's caravan, where they found Juliana trying to calm the two girls, who were almost hysterical.

"What's happened?" Sebastian asked

69

Joel, who was pacing up and down outside the caravan.

"I'm not sure," said Joel, running one hand over his black curls. "Something at the market upset them. Juliana's trying to find out what it was."

"We think there may be something strange happening in the land of the fairies," said Sebastian grimly. "The wish that we have been asked to grant was made by one of the fairy folk and we are on our way there now."

"You'd best come and talk to the girls," Joel replied.

They found the two girls inside the caravan, both still very upset. "Can you tell us what happened?" asked Sebastian after he'd explained who they were.

"We've been to the fairy market many times," said Luisa tearfully, "and it was always lovely; we would buy things or sell some of our own things and the fairies

would all be very kind to us."

"So what happened this time?" asked Maddie gently, taking Gabrielle's hand.

"They weren't the same," said Gabrielle, "they changed. They took some of our goods and gave us flowers for our hair but then they wouldn't let us go. They wanted us to stay there."

"You mean just for a while?" asked Maddie.

Luisa shook her head. "No," she said. "I think they wanted us to live with them."

"We told them we had our own home," said Gabrielle, "and that we had to go. They weren't friendly after that," she went on with a shudder. "They started jostling us – pushing, slapping and pinching."

"How terrible!" cried Maddie. "What happened then?"

"We tried to leave," said Luisa, "but they followed us and surrounded us."

"And these were fairy folk?" said

Reuben from the doorway of the caravan.

"Well, we thought they were," said Gabrielle uncertainly. "At first they seemed normal, just talking and laughing as usual, but then they. . ." She trailed off.

"Yes," prompted Maddie, "what then?"

"It was very strange – their faces seemed to change. Sometimes they would look their usual fair selves, and sometimes we'd glimpse pointed faces with sharp teeth and ears."

"Their expressions were evil," added Luisa, "and I'm sure I saw one whose tail swished as he walked, and some who had funny jagged wings."

"They don't sound like fairy folk to me," said Juliana, white-faced.

"What happened next?" asked Sebastian.

"They put us in the back of one of their carts," explained Luisa, "but one of them dropped the key as he was going to lock us up, and we managed to get away. We just ran and ran until we got back here."

"Did they follow you?" asked Reuben.

"We don't think so," said Gabrielle with a shudder.

"Well, you're safe now," said Sebastian, "but don't leave the encampment again until we know what's going on with the fairies."

"Oh, we won't," said the girls in unison.

"You both need to get to bed now," said Juliana, standing up.

The friends left the caravan and walked across to Reuben's wagon.

"I wonder why the fairies changed," said Maddie thoughtfully.

"Maybe they didn't change," said Sebastian, "maybe it's an enchantment. Maybe they weren't fairy folk in the first place but just pretending to be."

"Well, whatever it was it sounds really weird to me," said Maddie with a little shiver.

"Too right," agreed Zak. "But what I

73

want to know right now is where are we going to sleep. Did Joel say?"

Sebastian nodded. "Maddie, you are to sleep in the caravan of Juliana's sister Fenella – she was one of the dancers – and Reuben and I are sleeping in Reuben's wagon."

"What about me?" said Zak. "Don't I come into this?"

"Zak, you know you can sleep anywhere," said Sebastian with a sigh, "and let's face it, you usually do – even when you shouldn't."

"Oh, that's charming, that is," said Zak. "I suppose that wretched magpie has got a feather bed to sleep in!"

"He'll sleep with Reuben, as you know well," said Sebastian, "just as you will sleep beside me, like you always do."

"And we'll all be together in Reuben's wagon – is that what you're saying, eh?" Zak cocked his head on one side. "I don't

like the sound of that. No telling what that pesky bird might get up to in the middle of the night. . ."

"Zak, for goodness' sake!" sighed Sebastian.

"I'm only *saying*, that's all. . . So if it's all the same to you I think I'll sleep outside."

With the raven's grumbling still ringing in her ears, Maddie followed Fenella to her caravan with its pretty floral curtains and gleaming copper pots and pans. She was soon tucked up in bed, covered with the softest of patchwork quilts and in no time at all, tired out with the events of the day, she fell into a deep sleep.

"Maddie, Maddie."

Maddie opened her eyes, surprised to find that it was barely light and that Juliana was seated beside her on the bed, shaking her and calling her name.

75

"Oh," she said, struggling to sit up, "what is it? Have I overslept?"

"It's the girls," cried Juliana. "They are very ill. We don't know what to do."

"What do you think is wrong with them?" asked Maddie, pulling on her sweater.

"We don't know," said Fenella from the doorway. "But they are so ill they can barely move and old Meg who deals with any pills and potions we might need says it is beyond her and that she fears the girls might not recover."

"That's terrible!" cried Maddie, looking from Juliana to Fenella. "We need to speak to Sebastian."

"But what can he do?" asked Juliana, wringing her hands.

"Sebastian has magic," said Maddie.

Chapter Six

The Amethyst

Maddie hurried across the clearing to Reuben's wagon. It was very quiet but Zak was perched on the branch of a tree outside the wagon with his head under his wing, snoring loudly. Maddie peeped into the wagon and saw that Sebastian was still fast asleep but there was no sign of Reuben or Mishka. "Sebastian!" she called in a loud whisper and Sebastian stirred, opened his eyes and sat up.

"What is it?" he said when he caught sight of Maddie. "What's wrong, Maddie?" At that moment Zak awoke and flew down to join them, yawning loudly and protesting at the earliness of the hour.

"It's Luisa and Gabrielle," Maddie said urgently, "they've been taken ill in the night." Quickly she went on to explain to Sebastian what had happened. "The gypsies are afraid the girls might not survive," she finished. "Can you do something, Sebastian?" she added as he jumped to the ground from the back of the wagon.

"Time for a spot of magic, old son?" said Zak, cocking his head on one side.

"Maybe," Sebastian replied. "But first I think we need to pay a visit to Joel and his family."

The three of them hurried across the clearing to the large dark-green caravan decorated with painted garlands of flowers

that was home to Joel and his family.

They found Joel and Juliana beside themselves with worry and their two daughters lying in their beds, their faces deathly pale and their black curls tangled and matted.

"Have you any idea what could have caused this?" asked Sebastian.

"We suspect it has something to do with their visit to the fairy market," said Joel, his voice breaking and his huge shoulders heaving. "Old Meg fears there is no more that can be done for them. Can you help us, Sebastian?"

"Let me think about this for a moment," said Sebastian and with a deep sigh Joel went back into the caravan.

"You really are thinking about a spell, aren't you, old son?" said Zak.

"Yes," Sebastian replied, "I am. What do you think, Maddie?"

"Oh yes," Maddie spoke without

79

hesitation. "We must help them; the gypsies have been so good to us, welcoming us and sharing their food and their homes, but even if they hadn't, there are still two girls who are desperately in need of help, who might even die. I really can't think of a better use for a spell."

"We don't know what dangers we might have to face ahead," said Sebastian slowly.

"Well, we'd still have one spell left, wouldn't we?" said Maddie and when both Sebastian and Zak nodded, she added, "And I couldn't live with myself if something happened to those girls and we hadn't tried to help."

"In that case, if we're all agreed I'll go and get the ring. Start thinking about the spell, Maddie," said Sebastian over his shoulder as he made his way back to Reuben's wagon.

Maddie and Zak followed him, but only a moment later Sebastian appeared from

inside the wagon with his face pale and his eyes wide with shock.

"Sebastian!" Maddie exclaimed. "What is it, what's wrong?"

"The ring," he said.

"What about the ring?" asked Zak.

"It's gone!" said Sebastian.

"Waddya mean, gone?" Zak flapped his wings a couple of times.

"What I say." Sebastian looked wildly around the campsite, almost as if he expected to see the ring suddenly appear.

"When did you have it last?" Maddie asked anxiously.

"Last night," Sebastian replied. "I placed it beside me on the pallet that Reuben gave me to sleep on, but it isn't there now."

"So where is Reuben this morning?" asked Maddie.

"I don't know," said Sebastian distractedly. "You do realize what this means, don't you?" He looked frantically

 81

from Maddie to Zak, then back to Maddie again. "If the ring really is missing and can't be found we can't continue with the assignment!"

"What about the gypsy girls?" asked Maddie fearfully.

"We couldn't help them either," said Sebastian grimly. "We are powerless without the ring, it is our conductor of magic and without it the spells mean nothing. We'd have to go back to Zavania."

"Yep," said Zak, "and tell Zenith when he gets back from the desert not only that we couldn't grant the wish, but that we'd lost the amethyst ring as well. Oh boy, bagsy you be the one to tell him, Sebastian, old son!"

"If it comes to it, I shall tell him," said Maddie defiantly.

"Neither of you would tell him," said Sebastian. "The ring was my responsibility – I shall be the one to tell him."

"Hang on a minute," said Zak, "aren't we jumping the gun a bit here? Do we know for certain that the ring is well and truly lost?"

"Well, it certainly isn't where I left it," said Sebastian.

"Surely," Maddie said with a glance over her shoulder, "no one would have taken it?"

"We can't go round accusing the gypsy folk, can we?" snorted Zak. "Fine way to repay their hospitality that would be!"

"Here comes Reuben," said Maddie suddenly. "Let's ask him."

"So are you saying *he* might have taken it?" muttered Zak.

"No, of course not," said Maddie hotly, "but he might have seen it or something . . . it's worth asking him."

As Reuben walked towards them with Mishka perched upon his shoulder Sebastian explained what had happened. "I

83

just wondered if you remembered seeing it this morning," he finished.

Reuben shook his head. "I saw it last night when you took it off but I don't recall seeing it again this morning. I got up early to go for a walk. . ." He paused. "What happens if you can't find it?"

"We won't be able to grant the fairy's wish," Sebastian said simply, "neither will we be able to help Joel's girls."

"Joel's girls?" Reuben frowned.

"They are desperately ill." Maddie explained what had happened. "Sebastian was going to use one of the spells to help them," she went on, "but without the ring he can't do anything."

"That's terrible! Let's go and have another look inside the wagon," said Reuben, "it might have fallen on to the floor and rolled somewhere."

With that, Mishka flew on to the top of the wagon while Maddie, Sebastian and

84

Reuben climbed inside, where they carried out a thorough search around the pallets where Reuben and Sebastian had slept the night before.

"I can't see any sign of it," said Maddie after a while. "I know it's a bit dark in here but the amethyst is so bright I think we would see it if it was here."

"What will happen if you have to go back to Zavania without it?" asked Reuben as he straightened up from the corner where he had been poking about.

"It hardly bears thinking about," said Sebastian miserably, "but I reckon Zenith would probably banish me for ever."

"Oh Sebastian, no, surely not," cried Maddie. "That's awful. He wouldn't do that, would he?"

"That does seem a bit harsh," said Reuben, running one hand through his hair.

"It's all a question of responsibility

where Zenith is concerned," Sebastian replied, "and if I've failed in that responsibility. . ." He shrugged, leaving the sentence unfinished, then added, "The other thing we can't forget is that the ring is incredibly potent and if it fell into the wrong hands. . ." Once again he trailed off.

"Well," said Maddie firmly, "if Zenith does banish you, you can come home with me – I'm sure my mum would let you stay with us . . . and Zak," she added.

"Ah, Maddie." Sebastian shook his head sadly. "If only that were possible! But talking of Zak. . ." He glanced round the wagon and it was at that precise moment that there came the sounds of a huge commotion outside.

"What on earth. . . ?" exclaimed Reuben.

"Oh dear," said Sebastian, "I think we may have even more trouble on our hands."

The three of then jumped down from the wagon. The commotion, which appeared to be coming from the rear of the wagon, was growing louder, filling the air with fierce squawking, shrieking and screeching sounds.

"It sounds like Zak," muttered Maddie as they hurried round the wagon.

"That's what I'm afraid of," Sebastian replied out of the side of his mouth. "I only hope he hasn't upset any of the gypsies."

But the sight that met their eyes had nothing to do with any of the gypsies, although a few of them were watching in stunned silence as Zak the raven and Mishka the magpie fought together in an explosion of feathers that flew in all directions.

Within moments Sebastian and Reuben had separated the two birds, pulling them apart with stern words.

"What on earth do you think you are

doing?" demanded Sebastian as he held Zak, barely restraining him as the raven poked his beak and spat at the other bird.

"It's him!" Zak was beside himself with fury, an anger that Maddie had never seen in him before. "He's got it!"

"What are you talking about?" Sebastian looked across to where Reuben was trying to pacify his pet, talking soft words of comfort and gently smoothing his ruffled feathers.

"He's got the ring!" spat Zak. "Just let me get at him – the mangy bag of feathers."

"Zak, you can't go round making accusations like that. . ." Sebastian began.

"Well, ask him then! Go on, ask him."

But it was Reuben who asked the crucial question. Turning his head to speak to the magpie on his shoulder, he said, "Have you got the ring, Mishka? Did you take it?"

"Of course not!" the magpie protested. "Why would I?"

"Because that's what you magpies do," retorted Zak. "You see something that shines and you can't resist pinching it. And you bring bad luck as well!"

"Well! I can assure you that's an outrageous lie!" The magpie, hugely affronted, plumped out his chest feathers.

"So Joel's daughters may not recover," said Sebastian simply, and there was a terrible moment of silence as the friends looked at each other.

"Surely there's something else you can do," said the magpie suddenly. "You have magic spells, don't you?"

"They are useless without the ring to conduct the magic," said Sebastian.

"Mishka, are you *sure* you don't know anything about the ring?" said Maddie in sudden desperation. "I'm so worried about Luisa and Gabrielle."

"So am I," said Reuben grimly, "and if I find you did have anything to do with it,

Mishka, it won't only be Sebastian being banished – it will be you, too."

"You don't mean that," squawked Mishka haughtily, but for the first time Maddie thought she detected an uneasy glint in the magpie's eye.

"Don't I?" said Reuben dangerously. "Just try me."

There was a further silence, then the magpie rose from Reuben's shoulder and flew up to the top of the wagon where for a long moment and watched by them all, he poked about in a fold of the canvas cover. Seconds later, with a wary eye on Zak, he flew down again, back to the relative safety of Reuben's shoulder. But this time he carried in his beak an object that caught the rays of the early morning sunshine.

"Oh," gasped Maddie, "it's the ring, Sebastian!"

"Told you, didn't I?" squawked Zak in indignant triumph. "I said he'd pinched it –

thieving little varmint. Why will no one ever listen to me, that's what I want to know – it'd save a lot of trouble in the long run, I can tell you."

"Yes, all right Zak, not now," said Sebastian.

Zak hunched his wings but continued to throw out murderous looks in the magpie's direction as Reuben retrieved the ring from his beak and returned it to Sebastian.

91

"Please accept our apologies," said Reuben. He spoke quietly but Maddie suspected he was very angry underneath. "I can assure you the matter will be dealt with and fitting punishment carried out."

"What?" squawked Mishka in sudden alarm. "What do you mean?"

"I suspect you have other treasure up there in your hiding place," said Reuben and, as they all looked up to the roof of the wagon, the magpie hung his head.

"No wonder he didn't want me travelling up there," muttered Zak.

"I will confiscate whatever you have collected until you learn to behave," said Reuben, "and until we reach the land of the fairies I don't want you riding on my shoulder – you'll fly alongside."

At the tinker's words of judgement Mishka gave a squawk of misery.

"We need to move on," said Sebastian firmly, "since now that I have the ring

again we can perform the magic that will save Joel's girls. Maddie, we'll take a moment to remind ourselves of the spells, then we go into action."

Chapter Seven

The First Spell

Sebastian, Maddie and Zak gathered together outside Joel's caravan, watched from a distance by Reuben and Mishka the magpie, who glowered down at them from the roof of the wagon.

"Here we go then," said Sebastian, clearing his throat.

"Hey, you're not attempting to say this on your own, are you?" said Zak in alarm.

"Of course not," Sebastian replied with

an aloof expression, "Maddie helped me write the spell so it's only right she should say it with me."

"What you mean is," said Zak with a sly chuckle, "you can't remember a word of it and you'd be up the creek without her."

Ignoring the raven, Sebastian turned to Maddie. "Are you ready?" he asked, and if his hands were shaking just the tiniest bit it was only Maddie who noticed.

"Yes, of course," she replied firmly. Sebastian lifted his hand so that the rays of the early morning sun that filtered through the trees caught the amethyst in the ring on his finger. Together, he and Maddie began to recite the spell that they had so carefully composed in Zenith's turret room.

"Quilliban of Quincebar
Spread your Glow Both Near and Far

Quishta, Quando, Quillatist
Bring Purple Fire from Amethyst."

There was silence for a moment but as the amethyst began to glow more brightly, Sebastian said in a compelling voice, "Let Luisa and Gabrielle be restored to full health."

After he had spoken there was a further silence, the sort of silence where it seems as if everything becomes motionless, even the leaves on the trees, then suddenly there came a flash of purple fire.

Gradually everything went back to normal, the glow disappeared, a breeze rustled through the leaves and there came the sounds of everyday life as the gypsy folk went about their morning chores.

"How do you know it's worked?" Reuben looked doubtfully towards Joel's caravan where everything seemed still and quiet.

"Oh, it will have worked," said Maddie, "you need have no fear of that."

Sebastian chuckled. "You've come a long way, Maddie," he said. "Do you remember the time when even you doubted the spells would work?"

"No wonder at it when you could never remember them," said Zak, flapping his wings loudly. Then he abruptly stopped in mid-flap. "I say," he said, "get a load of that."

The other two looked where Zak was gesturing and were just in time to see Joel burst out of his caravan and leap down the steps.

"I can't believe it," he cried. "It's the girls – they've both opened their eyes, they're sitting up and asking for something to eat – they are so much better and only an hour ago they were . . . well, I thought we were going to lose them."

"Well, whaddya know," said Zak.

"You don't have to go right away, do you?" Joel looked from one to the other of them.

"We really do need to be getting on our way soon," said Sebastian.

"Come and see the girls first," said Joel.

They found the two gypsy girls sitting up in bed and drinking the soup their mother had prepared for them.

"They are much better," declared Juliana happily. "I don't know what you did, Sebastian, but whatever it was it worked. We will never be able to thank you enough."

"We are so pleased," said Sebastian, "and we have come to say goodbye. We have to go now into the land of the fairies and carry out our assignment."

"Oh, please be careful," said Luisa. Her voice still sounded weak after her ordeal. "There is something very wrong there and we fear you may be walking into deadly danger."

"We will take great care," said Sebastian, "have no fear."

They left the girls then and after saying their goodbyes to the gypsies, finally left the encampment.

"What do you think is happening in the land of the fairies?" asked Maddie, settling between Reuben and Sebastian as they began the last stage of their journey.

"I'm not sure," Reuben replied uneasily.

"Whatever it is, I don't like the sound of it," said Zak. Since they'd left the encampment Zak had taken to travelling on Sebastian's shoulder, which Maddie suspected was to annoy Mishka. The magpie had been forced to fly alongside the wagon as part of his punishment and was far from happy at having to do so.

"Neither do I," said Sebastian, "but at least we've been able to help the girls. Now we have to turn our thoughts once again to where we are going and to what we

have been asked to do."

"Yes," breathed Maddie, "we have to go on into the land of the fairies and grant Isabella's wish."

They travelled on through the gloomy depths of the forest until gradually the trees began to thin out and to Maddie's relief they emerged into bright sunshine once more. After that the path began to grow steep and Noah's hooves slipped at times on the sharp stones.

"I think we should get off the wagon and walk for a while," said Sebastian.

"Yes," Maddie agreed, "I was just going to say the same. Poor Noah is having to work twice as hard trying to pull our weight as well as the cart." Leaving Reuben at the reins, the friends clambered down from the wagon and began to trudge up the pathway on foot.

It was a long climb and as they walked

the sun beat down upon their backs and shoulders. When they paused for a rest Sebastian spoke in an irritable tone to Zak. "Do you have to ride on my shoulder?" he said. "You're jolly heavy, you know, especially in this heat."

"I have my reasons," said Zak loftily, casting haughty glances in the magpie's direction.

"I know you do," said Sebastian, "just as I know what those reasons are, but I would say you've more than proved your point, so how about you fly the rest of the way?"

"Eh? What?" The raven looked indignant. "Fly, you say? What, alongside that—"

"Yes, Zak," Maddie intervened, "why not? Mishka is still carrying out the terms of his punishment. I think if you were to fly alongside him for the last part of the journey if would give him a bit of encouragement. What do you say? Zak?"

Maddie leaned forward in order to look into the raven's face.

"Oh, I suppose so," scowled Zak at last. "Mind you," he added, "I'm not sure I'm going to forget what he did in a hurry."

"No one's asking you to, Zak. . ."

"And don't ask me to be his friend, because that's definitely out of the question." With that Zak rose up from Sebastian's shoulder, flapped his wings a few times then flew alongside the wagon on the opposite side to the magpie.

At last the pathway petered out on a ridge of rock. Here the wagon came to a halt and Sebastian and Maddie, both red in the face and out of breath, collapsed in a heap.

Maddie recovered first and sat up to peer beyond the ridge. What she saw almost took away what little breath she had left. "Oh, Sebastian," she gasped, "look, just look at that!"

Sebastian sat up and together the two of them gazed at the astonishing sight before them. Spread out below was a wide valley bounded on either side by gentle hills. In the valley, and surrounded by fields full of buttercups, daisies and bluebells, there was a small town. But it was a town like no other. There were many trees forming glens and dells while dotted here and there among the trees were quaint little houses of every colour imaginable, huddled together higgledy-piggledy beneath funny twisted chimneys of every shape and size. At the far end of the valley on a small hill stood a pink palace complete with turrets, moat and drawbridge. Little people, smaller than Maddie, flitted amongst the trees and flowers, going about their everyday business.

"Oh," said Maddie, clasping her hands together, "it's beautiful! Absolutely beautiful!"

 103

"Which is what you would expect from the land of the fairies," said Reuben. "It's a magical place."

"That's what makes it so hard to understand why they should want our help," said Sebastian slowly.

"The place must be in the grip of some evil that is stronger than their magic," said Reuben.

"Have you ever been here before, Sebastian?" asked Maddie.

"Once," he replied, "a very long time ago. Zenith brought me here to some sort of celebration, but I don't remember very much about it. You'll have to explain things to us, Reuben."

"Well," said Reuben, shielding his eyes from the sun with one hand and gazing down into the valley, "there's not really a lot to explain. The fairy folk go about their business very much like people do in any other town. Some of them live in the

little houses, others live in the trees. They make clothing, mainly from gossamer, and also shoes, jewellery and sweets, which they sell at their daily market. People come from miles around to attend the fairy markets. Then of course there are the factories over there behind the dell." Reuben pointed to a larger cluster of trees.

"What sort of factories?" breathed Maddie. The only factories she'd seen had been ugly looking buildings with tall chimneys, not at all like this magical place.

"Well, there's the factory of dreams," said Reuben. "Every good dream a child ever dreams is made there, and then there's the flower factory where flower fairies paint flowers with their beautiful colours. And, oh yes, there's the rainbow factory – they are kept pretty busy down there, especially in the rainy season." He paused, then went on. "The fairies' ruler, as

106

you know, is their queen, Tatiana, who lives over there in the palace." He pointed towards the pink building in the distance. "She is a fair and just ruler and all the fairy folk love her very much."

"So do you think that is where we should start," asked Maddie, "with a visit to the queen?"

"No." Reuben shook his head. "I don't think so. Like I said before, when I was last here there was no sign of Tatiana, nor did anyone mention her – which is highly unusual."

"Then maybe we need to find the fairy Isabella?" said Maddie.

"Actually," said Reuben, "I had another idea."

"Oh," said Zak innocently, "and what was that?"

"I thought that what was needed was for someone to go ahead and try and suss out the situation without being seen."

107

"So who did you have in mind – Sebastian?" Maddie asked.

Reuben shook his head. "I actually thought it might be better if we sent in the birds first."

"Eh? What!" spluttered Zak. "No way!"

"You object to going down there in advance?" asked Sebastian with a frown. "You're usually good at scouting, Zak."

"Oh, it's not the scouting I object to," said Zak with a scowl. "It's the company."

"He's frightened I'll be better than him and show him up," said Mishka, tossing his head.

"Why, you mangy creature," spat Zak, "I'll have you know I'm the best scout in the whole of Zavania."

"Looks like you're going to have to prove it, Zak," said Sebastian.

"In that case, I will," said Zak defiantly. "We'll go now."

108

"What?" squawked Mishka. "I was going to have a rest first."

"Well, if you're not up to it then you needn't come." Zak stretched his neck and flapped his wings before taking off and flying downward from the ridge into the valley below. After only a moment's hesitation Mishka followed him.

 Chapter Eight

The Market

Nervously they waited for the birds to return. "Do you think they'll be all right?" Maddie asked anxiously more than once.

Both Sebastian and Reuben hastened to reassure her. "They'll be fine," said Reuben.

But in spite of this, Maddie and, she suspected, Reuben and Sebastian as well, were all more than relieved when a sudden flapping of wings heralded the arrival of

the raven and the magpie. Surprisingly they returned together.

"Well?" demanded Sebastian. "What did you find out?"

"I say," panted Zak, "give a chap time to get his breath back."

"What did you see, Mishka?" asked Reuben, raising his arm so that the magpie could perch there.

"They're setting up the market," said the magpie, "and I saw Isabella!" No one could fail to notice the note of triumph in his tone.

"Did she see you?" asked Reuben.

"Oh yes," Mishka replied. "She was working in the shop where they repair wings. The window was open and I perched on the window sill. She saw me – she knew who I was."

"So what did she say?" asked Maddie, breathless with excitement.

"Not a lot." Mishka shrugged his wings.

"She put one finger to her lips as if to warn me not to say anything, and looked over her shoulder as if she was afraid of something or someone. Then she whispered very quietly, 'The wish?' I just nodded in reply but I figured that would let her know that help has arrived."

"Well done, Mishka," said Sebastian. "What about you, Zak, what did you find out?"

"Ah, well now, I just happened to meet up with a group of starlings that are passing through – I knew a couple of them from way back. . ."

"Zak, you haven't been gossiping again, have you?" demanded Sebastian while Mishka looked disdainful.

"You can call it gossiping if you like but I call it gleaning useful information. Of course, if you don't want to hear it. . ." Zak turned his back, clearly affronted.

This time it was Maddie who attempted

112

to calm ruffled feathers. "Come on, Zak," she coaxed, "we really do want to know what you found out – what did the starlings tell you?"

Zak sniffed but finally turned round again. "They said there was something strange going on over at Tatiana's palace," he said.

"Did they say what it was?" asked Maddie.

"They didn't know," Zak replied, "so I flew over to the palace."

"Did you see Tatiana?" asked Reuben curiously.

"Nope," Zak replied, "not a sign of her. And not only that, up close the place looks more like a prison than a palace – you can't see it from up here, but there's barbed wire around the entrance."

"So what on earth is happening?" said Maddie. "Where is the queen and why are the fairy folk so frightened?"

"That," said Sebastian grimly, "is what we have to find out. If the rest of you agree, I think we need to pay a visit and see for ourselves exactly what is going on. What do you say?"

"I agree," Reuben replied, "but we need to be very careful, bearing in mind what happened to the gypsy girls. . ."

"Hold on a moment," said Mishka suddenly, "I noticed something else."

"Go on," said Reuben when the magpie paused for effect.

"I noticed faces," said Mishka.

"What sort of faces?" Sebastian frowned.

"Faces that weren't fairy faces," said the magpie. "In unexpected places, among the crowd, or in a shop, perhaps peering out from under a hood. Suddenly there would be a face that didn't fit in with the others."

"So whose faces were they?" cried Maddie.

 114

"I don't know." The magpie shrugged. "All I know is they were evil faces, not like the fairy folk at all."

"Have you got any ideas, Reuben?" asked Sebastian.

"I might have," said Reuben slowly, "but I didn't want to alarm anyone unnecessarily."

"I think you need to say if you suspect anything," replied Sebastian, "then we might have some idea just what we are up against."

Reuben took a deep breath. "Everything so far seems to me to add up to one thing."

"And what's that?" said Sebastian.

"Not the Ice Queen," whispered Maddie, "please, not the Ice Queen again."

Reuben shook his head. "Not the Ice Queen – I was thinking. . ." Here he glanced around, then lowered his voice. "Goblins."

As he spoke Mishka gave a shriek and

Zak's neck feathers ruffled dramatically. "Shiver me timbers!" the raven muttered.

"Goblins!" echoed Maddie. "They are bad, horrible things, aren't they?"

"Just about as bad as you can get," said Reuben grimly.

"As bad as the Ice Queen?" Maddie shivered.

"Probably," muttered Zak. "They can be nasty, vicious little brutes."

"Not all of them," Sebastian interrupted. "I've known some goblins who came to see Zenith once and they seemed quite nice."

"That's true," Reuben agreed, "but the trouble is the really evil ones tend to band together and go about causing all kinds of trouble."

"We have people like that where I come from," said Maddie.

"We really do need to go down there and see for ourselves exactly what is

116

happening," said Sebastian. He looked round at the others. "Are you all ready?"

"Yes. . ." they all agreed, but they sounded dubious.

"In that case, we'll go now. I think it best if we travel in the wagon with you, Reuben – after all, they are used to seeing you so it might not arouse too much interest and hopefully by now the market might be getting busy with other people arriving. The other thing is, I think we all need to stick together – is that understood?"

"You're the boss," said Zak and the others nodded.

They travelled in near silence down the steep pathway into the valley and then into a tunnel of trees, some with hollow trunks where they glimpsed little staircases that led up to fairy houses among the branches. Some of the fairies came out of their homes

117

and smiled shyly at the friends as they passed, but just as quickly they would look away and go back inside their houses.

"It's like I said, that isn't like them at all," said Reuben. "By now we usually would have been invited into one of their houses. Something is obviously very wrong."

They trundled over the cobbles of the main street between rows of funny little houses with twisty chimneys and brightly coloured front doors.

"The market is always held in the main square," said Reuben. "I can't take the cart in there, but there's a large patch of grass behind the houses so I'll tether Noah there and we'll go on foot."

By the time the friends reached the square the fairy folk had almost finished setting out their stalls and the tiny alleyways were packed with ordinary people from other villages who had come in especially for the market.

 118

"I think we should be looking around for anything unusual," said Sebastian.

"Trouble is, we don't really know what usual is," said Maddie.

"Maybe not," Sebastian agreed, "but we can keep an eye out for anything alarming or untoward and, Reuben, we need you to look out for Isabella."

"There are some beautiful things on the stalls," said Maddie, stopping awhile to admire a rack of scarves of every colour of the rainbow. She found herself watching the fairy folk as they strolled amongst the stalls. They were smaller than Maddie and her friends, but were fine looking people with pale silvery hair, eyes as blue as a summer sky and soft gossamer wings. The smiles they bestowed upon Reuben and the friends were gentle but wary and it soon became evident that they were constantly on their guard, glancing over their shoulders as they set out and sold their goods.

The stalls were laden with merchandise of every kind: boots and shoes of the softest leather, garments of gossamer and silk and sparkling crystal jewellery. On one stall two fairies were painting flowers, roses in vibrant pink and deep purple iris; Maddie guessed they must be from the flower factory that Reuben had spoken of. On other stalls was produce – sweetmeats and jams and tray after tray of fruit. And it was fruit such as Maddie had never seen the like of before: blueberries the size of plums, soft juicy raspberries, pomegranates and lush red strawberries that made her mouth water.

And then gradually, eerily, just as Reuben had done, Maddie became uncomfortably aware of other faces amongst the market-goers and the gentle, beautiful faces of the fairy folk. These other faces were far from gentle or beautiful, these faces – just glimpses

really – were menacing, ugly, even wicked. At first these other faces were few and far between, peering out from under a pulled-down hood, half-hidden by a post or a length of fabric on a stall, but as time went on these instances seemed to become more frequent.

"Sebastian." Maddie tugged at his sleeve. "Have you seen them?"

"Oh yes," Sebastian replied, "I've seen them all right – they are everywhere! It's just as you said, Reuben." He turned towards the tinker, who was right behind him with the magpie reinstated on his shoulder. "Can you see Isabella anywhere?" he added quietly.

"Yes." Reuben nodded. "She's over there – behind that stall. She's seen us. Why don't you and Maddie go over and speak to her and I'll stay here with the birds. Maybe that way we won't attract too much attention."

 121

"Good idea," said Sebastian. "Come on, Maddie."

"Watch yourselves," Zak muttered out of the corner of his beak. "Pesky little devils are everywhere."

Together, Sebastian and Maddie approached the stall that Reuben had indicated. Isabella stood behind the stall but on seeing the friends approach she moved out. She was as beautiful as the rest of her people with pale silvery hair and almost translucent skin, while her dress, made of the sheerest gossamer in shades of blue and green, reminded Maddie of spiders' webs on a September morning.

Sebastian pretended to be examining some of the goods on the stall, but while he did so he spoke quickly and urgently in a quiet undertone. "We are here to help you, Isabella," he said, "and we think we have identified your problem. I know you can't say too much, but just tell us, have

122

they overtaken the whole town?"

Isabella nodded at the same time as picking up a purple shawl and holding it up as if Sebastian or Maddie might be interested in buying it. "They are everywhere," she whispered.

"And Tatiana?" murmured Sebastian.

"They have her held captive; they take everything we earn as a ransom – but it is never enough."

123

Sebastian drew in his breath sharply at her words, then, with a quick glance in her direction, he said, "Don't worry, we are here now, all will be well."

"Oh please," whispered Isabella, "please, please be careful – you don't know what they're like ... move away now, they mustn't see us talking."

Sebastian nodded and together he and Maddie moved away from Isabella and nonchalantly began examining goods on other stalls.

Maddie was on the point of asking Sebastian what he intended doing next, but when she looked around she saw that the crowd around the stalls had grown more dense and that Sebastian was separated from her by at least three people.

"Oh ... Sebastian," she called, but because of the noise around them he didn't seem to hear her. She began to try to move forward in order to reach him, but quite

suddenly those around her began to push and jostle her. Growing frightened, she pushed back but this just seemed to make them worse; the pushing grew harder as first one and then another pinched her arms and in a flash she was reminded of what had happened to the gypsy girls. In one last desperate attempt to reach Sebastian, she pitched headlong into the crowd but those around her didn't give way by so much as an inch, and before she knew what was happening she was plunged into sudden and terrifying darkness as what felt like a thick blanket was thrown over her head.

Desperately, she tried to struggle but her arms were pinioned by her sides and with the thick cloth covering her nose and mouth she felt as if she was going to suffocate. She was dimly aware of sounds – shouting and thuds, squawking from Zak and screeching from Mishka – then it felt

as if she was being lifted from the ground and bundled into something that felt hard to her hands and knees.

By this time she was quite terrified, unbearably hot and in serious danger of choking. Even as she despaired of what she could do next, she heard cries and whatever it was she had been thrown into began to move, rapidly gathering speed. Blindly, Maddie tried to grope in the darkness to find out whether Sebastian was with her but her searching fingers only encountered a hard wooden surface.

Whatever it was that Maddie was in bumped and jerked over the cobbles as it continued to travel at speed, swaying alarmingly from side to side amidst cries and shouts, until at last, mercifully, it stopped.

Gradually, cautiously, Maddie found she was able to pull the thick cover from her head. The sunlight caused her to blink as

she emerged like a little mole, trying to adjust her eyes to the sudden bright light.

To her horror she found she was in some sort of cage made of bamboo canes while the cage itself was on a donkey cart. Fearfully, she peered around. There was no sign of Sebastian, Zak or Reuben and Mishka – instead, a group of short, squat figures clad in hooded grey robes were sitting in a circle on the ground a little distance from the cart.

"Hey!" she shouted and the figures looked up. "Let me out of here at once!"

The figures began cackling and rubbing their hands together and as Maddie caught sight of their faces her heart sank, for these were the evil faces she'd glimpsed among the crowd, the faces that had terrorized the gentle fairy folk so much. The faces that Reuben believed belonged to goblins.

Chapter Nine

Captured!

Two of the goblins left their circle and moved, part hobbling, part running, across to the cage that held Maddie. One of them picked up a stick and began poking it through the bars at her and both of them began to taunt her. Maddie shank back into the corner of the cage in terror. She had been about to demand once more that they let her go but she realized that they appeared to be talking some sort of

gibberish full of grunts and snarls, and a language she'd never heard before. She ended up doubting that they would understand her if she couldn't understand them. She could see their faces clearly now and they really were quite hideous, with long noses and chins sprouting tufts of hair and warts, pointed ears, and the most evil of expressions in their beady eyes. And when she saw that one of them had a long pointed tail that twitched and rasped on the dry ground she was reminded once again of the words of the gypsy girls.

After a time the two goblins seemed to grow tired of taunting Maddie and returned to the others, where they all set up a wave of demon-like laughter.

Desperately, she peered round at her surroundings. They appeared to be in some sort of courtyard with high stone walls on either side. Apart from the noise that the

goblins were making it was otherwise very quiet, so Maddie guessed they must be some distance from the hustle and bustle of the marketplace.

Oh, where was Sebastian? Would he be able to rescue her or had he been captured as well? She knew he had magic and that he would use it if he really had to, but there was only one spell left and they still had so much to do. Suddenly Maddie wanted to cry. She could feel a lump the size of an egg in her throat and hot angry tears prickled the backs of her eyelids. She didn't want to be here at all. She wanted to be at home, tucked up in her own bed, not in this strange land overrun by evil goblins.

Maybe, she thought as she tried to swallow, maybe this really was just a dream and if she closed her eyes it would go away. She squeezed her eyes tightly shut then, and quite suddenly, realized that she could

no longer hear the snarling and demon-like laughter of the goblins.

Could she have been right? Was it all a dream? Would she be in her own bed if she opened her eyes? Would it be dark with just the little glow of the night-light that her mum kept burning on the landing? Her heart gave a little leap of hope and at last she dared to open her eyes.

She nearly wept from sheer disappointment, for instead of being in her bedroom she found she was still in the courtyard. But this time she appeared to be alone and the menacing group of goblins had disappeared. She sat upright and gripped the bars of the cage, when from somewhere to the left of her she heard a sound.

"Psst!"

She peered round but at first she couldn't see anything. Then the sound came again.

"Psst! Down here!"

She looked down, and there between the donkey's hooves she saw a familiar and very welcome sight. "Zak!" she cried in relief.

"Sshh! For goodness' sake!" he muttered. "We don't want those pesky little varmints to cotton on, do we?"

"Oh, no," said Maddie, "no, of course not."

"OK," said Zak. "So we'll keep this brief. First of all, are you all right?"

"Yes, I think so." Maddie nodded. "But I don't know what they're going to do with me."

"Well, it's obvious you've been kidnapped – and probably held to ransom," said Zak.

"What!" squeaked Maddie.

"Stands to reason." Zak shrugged his wings. "It's what they do – we've sussed that much already."

"But I haven't got any money," said Maddie in desperation, "I can't pay any ransom."

"They probably figure Sebastian can with the size of the ring he's wearing."

"Is Sebastian all right?" Maddie asked frantically.

"They knocked him for six when they grabbed you—"

"What!"

"Yep." Zak chuckled. "Out cold he was, but me and the magpie caused a diversion and Reuben went in and got him out."

"But is he all right?" demanded Maddie.

"Haven't a clue." Zak shrugged again. "I chose to follow the donkey cart to see where they were taking you."

"But. . ."

"Don't worry," said Zak with a sigh, "I'm sure he'll be OK."

At that moment there came sounds from the far end of the courtyard. "Oh,"

cried Maddie, "they are coming back, they mustn't find you here, Zak."

"OK," said Zak, "but whatever happens, don't worry – we'll get you out."

"But how. . . ?"

"I'd better be off," said Zak grimly as a group of goblins came into sight, some leaping and hobbling, one or two even flying.

"Wait, Zak, where am I?" asked Maddie in sudden desperation. "Where have they brought me?"

But there was no time for Zak to answer, for the goblins reached the cart at that moment and this time they threw the blanket not over Maddie's head but over the entire cage. The last thing she saw before she was plunged into darkness again was the raven as he flapped his great wings and took off into the air.

Maddie felt as if the cage was being lifted from the back of the donkey cart,

amid many grunts and groans from the goblins, and was then carried for a fair distance. If only Zak had had time to tell her where she was, she thought in despair, as they bumped and jolted along. He'd said Sebastian had been hurt when he'd tried to come to her rescue, knocked out even, and although he'd gone on to say that Sebastian was all right she had the horrible feeling that he had only been trying to make her feel better. Even as she fretted and worried in the midst of her own terror, the cover over the cage was suddenly dragged off and Maddie realized that it had caught on the rough surface of a wall. The goblins carrying the cage didn't stop to retrieve it so at least Maddie was able to see where they were going. Not that there was very much to see. They appeared to be in a gloomy corridor, the only light coming from flaming torches set in iron brackets in the stone walls, and as they travelled at a

prisingly rapid pace Maddie noticed ickles of water glistening down the walls.

At last they stopped and the goblins opened a small wooden door set in the stonework. Pushing the cage right up against the opening they proceeded to remove one end of the cage. All Maddie could see beyond the open doorway was darkness and she shrank back into one corner of the cage in fear. Then to her dismay the goblins began pushing her through the bars and prodding her with sticks, just as they had done before, and all the while keeping up their nasty snarling and grunting noises.

"All right," cried Maddie, "there's no need for that. I'm going!" In spite of being frightened she was also angry at the way they were treating her. Whether or not they understood her Maddie didn't know, but they fell back at the sound of her voice. They watched as, with as much dignity as

the small cage would allow, she moved into the darkness beyond the small wooden door, relieved to get away from the goblins.

Maddie didn't think she would ever, as long as she lived, forget the sound that the door made as it slammed shut behind her. She half turned to protest, but her last glimpse of the goblins was of two of their evil, grinning faces as they peered in through a grill set in the door.

She stood very still and swallowed. The lump was back in her throat again and this time the tears didn't just prick at her eyelids, they began to roll unchecked down her cheeks. She didn't really have any doubt that Sebastian and Zak would somehow come to her rescue, but at that precise moment she felt very lonely indeed.

It was much darker than in the passage outside. The only light came from the grill in the door and from a second iron grill high up on the far wall, which looked as if

it might be some sort of window with a tantalizing glimpse of daylight beyond.

As her eyes cleared of tears and grew accustomed to the gloom and her ears to the silence, Maddie very gradually became aware that the silence wasn't quite as total as she had at first thought. There was a slight rustling sound and it seemed to be coming from the far corner beneath the window.

She was not alone.

She stiffened, straining her ears. The rustling grew louder and this time was accompanied by a little sob. Hardly daring to breathe, Maddie stepped forward and peered into the darkness. From the meagre light that filtered through the bars she could see a mound in the corner, which even as she watched began to move.

Maddie gulped, her eyes widening with terror as she tried to imagine whatever it

might be, but as the sobbing continued she was moved to pity.

"Hello?" she said, and when the rustling and sobbing abruptly stopped she went on. "Don't be afraid, I'm not going to hurt you. I'm a prisoner in this awful place as well."

There was silence for a further few minutes, then slowly, very slowly, the mound began to move and Maddie braced herself to face whatever it might be. And then her breath caught in her throat as a figure emerged and stood up before her, a figure of a girl with dirty tattered clothes and long pale hair that had surely once been beautiful but which was now was matted and unkempt and hung about her face and shoulders in long strands. Just visible were a pair of wings, fragile and gossamer thin, but delicately coloured in rainbow shades.

"Oh," cried Maddie, "who are you?"

139

She had a feeling she knew who this was but she needed to be sure.

"I am Tatiana," the girl said, confirming Maddie's suspicions, "I am the Queen of the Fairies."

"Oh, Your Majesty!" said Maddie, and gave a little curtsy. "I'm so pleased I've found you."

"But who are you?" said Tatiana. "And why are you a prisoner here?"

"My name is Maddie, and I'm here because one of your fairies made a wish that you might all be free again."

"One of my fairies?" asked Tatiana curiously.

"Yes," Maddie explained, "Isabella."

"Ah, Isabella! She is a Tooth Fairy but she is also one of my ladies-in-waiting," said Tatiana with another little sob, "and she is very dear to me. But how did she manage to get a message to you without the goblins finding out?"

 140

"She spoke to Reuben the Tinker," said Maddie breathlessly, "and when he told her he was going to Zavania she asked him to take her wish to Zenith the WishMaster."

"Zenith?" said Tatiana. "Is he here?"

Maddie shook her head and then, sensing Tatiana's disappointment, she hurried. "But Sebastian is here, he is Zenith's Junior WishMaster and he has magic to grant the wish."

"He will need to be very careful," said Tatiana. "The goblins are not only evil, full of wickedness and cunning, but they are also here in vast numbers. And their leader, Griffon the Lord Goblin, is with them. They have taken over everything in the town. They took me prisoner and stole my magic wand, which is my conductor of magic and controls the magic of all my fairies – we are powerless without it. They have held me to ransom but no matter how hard my poor people work they can never

141

make enough money to pay them off."

"Where are we?" asked Maddie, looking around. "What is this place?"

"This is my own home," said Tatiana, "my palace. We are in part of the basement cellars, which are used to store our produce. They sent all my servants back to the town to work and have kept me in here while they have taken over my beautiful palace."

"Don't worry," said Maddie, "Sebastian has magic – he had two spells, but we had to use one on our way here." She went on to explain to Tatiana about how Luisa and Gabrielle had visited the fairy market and had been captured, how they had escaped but had then fallen very ill that night.

"We think it must have been something to do with the goblins," Maddie went on, "but they were so ill that Sebastian had to use a spell so that they would recover."

"It would definitely have been the goblins," said Tatiana. "They have magic of their own, perhaps the goblins planned to hold the girls to ransom – they would have overrun the gypsy camp, just as they have my land – and then when they found the girls had escaped they put a spell on them." Looking curiously at Maddie, she said, "But you haven't told me yet who you are."

"I'm a friend of Sebastian and of Zak the raven," Maddie replied. "I come from . . .

the Other Place. We were in the market and the goblins captured me and brought me here."

"Ah," said Tatiana. She paused. "So how do you think Sebastian's magic will work?"

"I'm not actually sure at the moment," Maddie admitted fearfully, "but you really mustn't worry because what I do know is that Sebastian will find a way."

"Well, I hope so," said Tatiana sadly, "for all our sakes. We have long been at odds with the goblins, trying to put right the evil they have done, but their power is great and truly terrifying. I fear it will take very strong magic to overcome them."

"Sebastian has strong magic," said Maddie, with more confidence than she was feeling.

Chapter Ten

The Secret Passage

As the sun went down and twilight descended, a large crescent moon rose over the land of the fairies and Maddie and Tatiana dozed in their prison cell. They had been given a supper of chunks of mouldy bread and a pitcher of water, but whereas Tatiana, who was quite obviously ravenous, fell upon hers Maddie couldn't eat a thing.

She didn't know how Sebastian would

set about trying to rescue her, she only hoped he would do so quickly. She didn't think she would sleep a wink on the rough straw on the cellar floor, but she must have done for she woke suddenly with a start.

Something had woken her – but what? She peered around the cell, which was lit only by shafts of moonlight; Tatiana appeared to be asleep in her corner, so it hadn't been her who had made a noise. Maddie turned her gaze towards the door, fearful that the goblins were outside and about to burst in.

"Maddie!"

Someone had called her name. Wildly, she looked round again.

"Maddie, Maddie, up here."

She scrambled to her feet, crossed the cell and peered up at the small grating set high in the stone wall. "Sebastian. . . ?" she breathed. "Is that you?"

 146

"Yes," he replied. "Maddie, are you all right?"

"Yes, I am," she said. "Tatiana is here as well," she added, then she heard a sound and Tatiana came to stand beside her.

"Your Majesty," said Sebastian, clearly moved at seeing the queen of the fairies in such lowly circumstances.

"We're going to try and get you out, Maddie," Sebastian went on after a moment.

"But how will you do that?" asked Maddie desperately.

"I'll use the spell," Sebastian replied. "We'll say it together now."

"No," said Maddie quickly, "don't do that. You can't do that, you'll have nothing left to grant the wish and you have to free the fairy folk, Sebastian, you really do. They are in terrible trouble – you've no idea how evil those goblins are."

"I know," said Sebastian, "but I will

 147

attempt to use the spell to free everyone at the same time."

"Wait," said Tatiana, "that is too much to ask of one spell, Sebastian. If I could retrieve my magic wand, then maybe I could help you."

"Where is it?" asked Sebastian urgently.

"The Lord of the Goblins has it," Tatiana replied. "It is my conductor of magic, you will understand what that means, Sebastian – without it I have no magic powers at all, but if we could get out of this cell. . ."

"Have you any idea where the keys are kept?" asked Sebastian.

"They are on a hook outside the door," Tatiana replied.

"But how can we get them?" said Sebastian. "The goblins are everywhere."

"I've had an idea," said Maddie suddenly, "I'm not sure whether it will

 148

work but it's worth a try. Is Zak with you?"

"Yes, he is," Sebastian replied. "Reuben and Mishka are here as well. What's your idea, Maddie?"

"If Zak could squeeze through these bars and then through the grill on the door, he could get the keys from the hook outside, and we could let ourselves out."

"How would you get past the goblins?" asked Sebastian doubtfully.

"I know a way," Tatiana replied calmly. "There's a secret passage which I doubt even they will have found; it runs from a room near the kitchens and comes up in my throne room where my magic wand is kept. We will have to be very careful but I think we could do it."

Sebastian came to a swift decision. "All right. It's worth a try. Zak?"

"OK," muttered the raven, who had obviously been perched somewhere

149

alongside Sebastian and listening to the conversation. "Here we go. Nothing to it. Easy-peasy."

There followed much straining and grunting as Zak tried to squeeze himself between the bars.

"I don't think it's going to work, Zak," said Sebastian at last, and Maddie felt her heart sink. "You've put on too much weight."

"Eh? What? Don't be stupid, of course I haven't," said Zak as, puffing and panting, he made another attempt.

"I keep telling you not to eat all those titbits they put out for the castle birds," grumbled Sebastian. "Well, there's nothing for it, we'll have to think of something else."

"I could do it," said a voice from behind Sebastian and Zak, and Maddie caught a quick glimpse of Mishka.

"Oh, no you don't!" muttered Zak

furiously and he struggled once again to fit between the bars.

"Zak, stop it!" ordered Sebastian sternly. "You'll just get stuck and then we'll be in even worse trouble. Far better to let Mishka try, he's smaller than you."

Amidst much muttering and grumbling, Zak stood back and a few seconds later the magpie flew into the cell and Maddie pointed him in the direction of the grill in the top of the door.

In no time at all the magpie was back with the keys, which Maddie took from his beak. "Thank you, Mishka," she whispered, stroking his handsome feathers while the magpie arched his neck in glee.

"Where shall we meet you?" asked Sebastian urgently as Mishka flew back to rejoin Reuben, who was waiting quietly in the shadows.

"There are glass doors that lead from the throne room on to the terrace,"

Tatiana replied, "and opposite the terrace is thick shrubbery – wait there for us."

"Very well," said Sebastian, "but please, please, be careful."

"Yes," said Maddie, "and you be careful too."

Cautiously Tatiana inserted the key into the lock and turned it, the door swung open and together she and Maddie emerged from their prison into the corridor. Peering from left to right they found to their relief there was no sign of any goblins. Maddie had feared that they would find one or two on guard outside the cell but the corridor was empty.

"Come on," said Tatiana, "this way." Together they sped along the corridor, took a series of complicated left-, then right-, then left-hand turnings, followed by a flight of steps that took them out of the cellars and into the palace itself. Once,

they heard the now familiar demon-like laughter coming from a room nearby and a little later they heard another noise, at which Tatiana grabbed Maddie's arm and pulled her into the deep shadows of a recess in the wall. She was only just in time, for as they stood there, quaking, a group of goblins passed by just inches away, so close in fact that had Maddie reached out her hand she could have touched them.

"They've taken over almost every room of the palace," whispered Tatiana after the goblins had passed by. "But it looks like at the moment they are all on their way to the banqueting hall – which is good because it just might let us get out of here without being seen."

They carried on through the palace corridors until they reached a room with a large inglenook fireplace. Fortunately the room was deserted. "Over here," said

153

Tatiana, crossing the room. Moving inside the fireplace she reached up and pulled a lever that was hidden from the view of anyone who happened to be in the room. As she did so, a huge slab of stone slid to one side. "Come on, quickly." Tatiana beckonèd to Maddie, who followed her through the opening. Once on the other side, Tatiana slid the stone back into place.

They found themselves in yet another passage but this one was smaller and even darker with no flaming torches and not even a glimmer of light to guide them. "Don't be afraid," said Tatiana. "Just keep very close behind me."

It smelt damp, felt desperately cold and seemed endless with several twists and turns. But just when Maddie feared they were never going to reach the end, Tatiana suddenly stopped and Maddie almost careered into the back of her.

Once again, Tatiana found the secret

154

mechanism in a wall of stone and as the wall swung open they were greeted by the gentle pearly light of dawn, which stole into the room through the large floor to ceiling windows. At one end of the room was a dais with a golden throne padded with red velvet. As Maddie stepped blinking into the light, Tatiana slid the secret door into place.

"This is my throne room," whispered Tatiana. "My wand is usually kept beside the throne." Gracefully, she flapped her beautiful gossamer wings and flew across the room towards the dais, where she alighted in front of the throne and began her search, lifting the velvet curtains behind the throne and even peering under the throne itself.

"It isn't there!" she exclaimed at last and Maddie could hear the anguish in her voice.

"Perhaps the Goblin Lord has taken it for himself," said Maddie.

"It won't be any good to him," said Tatiana, "because the wand only works for me."

At that moment there came a noise from outside the throne room, a noise like the tramping of feet.

"They're coming!" cried Maddie. "The goblins are coming!"

"Quickly," said Tatiana, flying down to join Maddie and taking her hand. "We need to get out of here." They sped across the highly polished floor of the throne room and within seconds Tatiana had led them out on to the terrace through one of the glass doors.

On the terrace they paused for a moment, looking from right to left, then a slight movement in the bushes caught Maddie's eye. "Oh look," she breathed, "there's Zak!"

"Careful," said Tatiana, "we need to be sure there's no one else around."

At that moment a figure appeared from behind the bushes and beckoned furiously to the two of them. "There's Sebastian," said Maddie in relief. "We'll be safe now." Taking Tatiana's hand, they rushed towards the dense foliage where they found not only Sebastian and Zak but also Reuben and Mishka.

Maddie almost fell into Sebastian's arms and he hugged her fiercely. "Thank goodness you are all right," he said. "We have been so worried about you."

"That's putting it mildly," said Zak with a sigh.

"But what about you?" said Maddie. "Zak said you'd been knocked out and I didn't have a chance to ask before—"

"Oh, it was nothing." Sebastian shrugged. "I'm OK, thanks to Reuben – he came in and got me away from them." Turning to Tatiana, he bowed. "Your Majesty," he said. "I trust you haven't been harmed?"

She shook her head but in the cold light of day Maddie could see just what effect Tatiana's ordeal had had upon her. There were dark circles beneath her eyes and her clothes hung in tatters from her thin body.

"They will pay for this," said Sebastian grimly. "Their evil ways are at an end. But tell me, did you recover your magic wand?"

Tatiana sadly shook her head. "It wasn't there and without it I am powerless."

"Don't worry," said Sebastian quietly, "we'll find it for you. And in the meantime I have my own magic."

"But first," said Sebastian, "I would like us all to get well away from this place so that no one gets hurt. I suggest we all try to make our way back to the town."

"Good idea," said Reuben. "With a bit of luck the goblins might still all be in bed – they're a lazy lot at the best of times."

"Well, we'll hope so," agreed Sebastian. "It'd be just our luck they're up early

this morning," muttered Zak. Maddie thought the raven seemed rather grumpy and she guessed he was still in a sulk over Mishka being the one who'd retrieved the keys and not him.

"They are up," said Tatiana. "Most of them were in the banqueting hall and Maddie and I heard some of them outside the throne room. And if they've taken food to the cellar they will have discovered we've escaped."

"In which case we really do need to get a move on," said Sebastian. "Now, what I suggest we do is make our way round to the side of the palace, then with a bit of luck we can make a dash down the hill to the town."

The others all agreed and within moments the little band had cautiously left the shelter of the bushes and crossed the terrace. Quickly and quietly they made their way round the corner of the palace.

But there they were forced to stop dead in their tracks, for they were faced by a group of goblins spread out in a long, menacing line barring their way.

"Jeepers!" squawked Zak.

"Oh no!" gasped Maddie. "Oh, just look at them, Sebastian, they look so evil."

Tatiana seemed to sway and Reuben put an arm around her to both protect and support the fragile queen of the fairies.

The goblins began to inch towards them, jeering and catcalling, sneering and snarling as they came. Some of them wore hoods pulled down over their faces, others swished their tails and a couple hunched their backs to reveal vicious-looking spiked wings.

"They're so horrible," whimpered Maddie. "What are we going to do?"

"Back the other way," said Reuben suddenly. "If we can get back into the cover of the bushes we might be able to escape that way."

They all turned and sped back across the terrace but long before they reached the bushes a second band of goblins appeared from the other direction, cutting off their escape route. The friends stopped in dismay and Maddie was just thinking that this was as bad as it could get when she looked up and saw on the steep banks behind the bushes not just a handful of goblins, but dozens and dozens of them, hobbling, running or flying towards them. And when she turned and looked up at the palace it was to find that they lined the battlements and hung from the turrets, while on the terrace steps stood a goblin who was even more terrifying than all the others.

He appeared taller than most of them and wore a hood and tunic of gold chain mail. His features were twisted and ugly, his expression cunning and evil. In one hand he held a sword and in the other he

held triumphantly aloft a wand that glittered in the early morning light.

"It's Griffon," breathed Tatiana, "the Goblin Lord."

In despair Maddie turned to Sebastian. "Oh," she cried, "Sebastian, we must use the spell!"

Chapter Eleven

The Wish is Granted

"Oh my giddy aunt!" squawked Zak. "Come back, Ice Queen, all is forgiven."

"You don't mean that, Zak," muttered Sebastian grimly.

"What? No, I don't suppose I do," Zak agreed. "But having said that, I would say that what we have here is a pretty desperate situation, old son, wouldn't you?"

"Absolutely," Sebastian agreed and

163

then, drawing himself up to his full height and flicking his cloak back over one shoulder, he added, "and desperate situations call for desperate measures. The time has come. Maddie, are you ready?"

"Oh yes," Maddie replied. "Just say the word."

"I hope you lot know what you're doing," said Reuben nervously, while Mishka, much to Zak's delighted disgust, hid himself beneath his master's coat.

"Right," said Sebastian, "let's go." Lifting his right hand upwards so that the rays of the morning sun caught the amethyst in the ring, he and Maddie began to recite the second spell.

"Quineria over Quinewel
Bring Magic from this Jewel
Questa, Quosta, Queen
Bathe the Land in Purple Sheen."

Then in a loud voice Sebastian said. "By the power of the amethyst, let our foe be turned to stone."

As he finished speaking Maddie held her breath, only too aware that the goblins were creeping even closer, so close that she could now see every detail of their crafty expressions, their hideous wicked faces.

At first nothing happened and Maddie could see Reuben getting agitated but she knew, given just one moment of time, that Sebastian's magic would work.

Sure enough, a purple glow began to gradually settle upon the land, bathing everything in its unusual light.

The goblins stopped in their tracks and peered around them in astonishment and Tatiana gripped Maddie's hand.

And then a very curious thing began to happen. The goblins stopped creeping forward and grew very still, the catcalls

and the snarling ceased and there was silence, a silence so complete that the friends hardly dared to move or to utter a sound.

It was Zak who eventually broke the silence. "Well bless my soul!" he exclaimed. "Will you look at that! They're turning to stone – all of 'em! You've surpassed yourself this time, old son, and that's a fact."

Even as he spoke there was a sudden terrible crash and two of the goblins who had been flying suddenly fell to the ground. In their new stone-like condition, they shattered into a thousand pieces while all around them their companions remained where they stood, in whatever pose they had been in, their faces caught for all time in evil grimaces.

After a while the purple glow faded away and the friends looked at each other with a mixture of relief and amazement. "I don't think," said Sebastian, turning to

166

Tatiana, "that you'll ever be bothered by goblins again." As he spoke he looked up, and when the others followed his gaze they saw several stone goblins on the battlements staring down with sightless eyes like hideous gargoyles.

"I might just leave those there," said Tatiana quietly, "to serve as a warning to any other creatures who might have the same idea as this particular bunch of goblins. But first I need to retrieve my wand."

"I'll get it for you," said Reuben, and he ran forward to the steps where Griffon the Goblin Lord stood in his stone-like trance, his sword in pieces on the ground at his feet, Tatiana's wand still in his stone fist. Reuben grasped the wand but it wouldn't budge. He tried again but still nothing happened.

"I think," said Sebastian, "you'd better try, Your Majesty."

167

Tatiana stepped forward and, watched by the others as they held their breath, she walked slowly to the terrace steps where she looked steadily into the sightless eyes of the Goblin Lord. Then, reaching out her hand, she effortlessly slid her wand from his grasp. Turning to the friends she held the wand aloft. "Thanks to all of you, my magic is back where it belongs," she said, and a tear slid down her cheek.

Unable to control herself Maddie ran forward and hugged Tatiana.

"Well, that's that then," said Zak, but even he looked emotional.

"I will never be able to thank you enough," said Tatiana. "And I want you to know that if ever you are in need of my magic, for any reason, you only have to say the word."

The fairy folk of the town ran out to meet them, overjoyed to be free from the wicked

rule of the goblins. There was a touching reunion between Tatiana and Isabella when Tatiana thanked her friend for risking her own life in asking Reuben to take the wish to Zavania.

"And now we have to go back to Zavania," said Sebastian.

"And I need to go on to my own land," said Reuben and Maddie thought he sounded almost sad, while even Zak and Mishka seemed to be on much better terms than they had once been.

"How will you get home?" asked Isabella anxiously, concerned for the friends who had helped her.

"I haven't quite thought that one out yet," Sebastian admitted.

"Can't you use another spell?" asked Isabella.

Sebastian shook his head. "We only had two spells with us and we've used them both."

169

"You need not worry about that," said Tatiana and they all turned to look at her. "Come back to the palace with me – all of you – for some refreshment and then I will arrange to transport you back to Zavania. You come too, Reuben," she added, so there would be no confusion. But the tinker shook his head.

"Thank you, but no," he said, "I really do need to be on my way."

Reluctantly, they all took their leave of Reuben and Mishka, then watched sadly as the tinker strode away, playing a haunting little melody on his mouth organ, his hat at a jaunty angle and the magpie on his shoulder.

"I shall miss him," said Maddie, "and Mishka."

"I say, steady on," muttered Zak, but he didn't sound very convincing.

"Maybe we'll meet up with them again some day," said Sebastian.

Together with a crowd of fairy folk from the town, the friends, Isabella and Tatiana began to make their way back through the town and up the hill to the palace. Everywhere they looked there were stone goblins, some peering out of doorways, some on rooftops and others around the stalls in the early-morning marketplace.

"What on earth will you do with them all?" Maddie asked Tatiana curiously.

"I shall use my magic to have them transported back to their own land," Tatiana replied firmly.

"Will you ever change them back again?" asked Zak.

"I haven't decided yet," Tatiana replied, "but if I do, it won't be for a very, very long time indeed."

After a delicious meal in the banqueting hall of Tatiana's palace, and waited on by her courtiers, Sebastian rose to his feet. "I

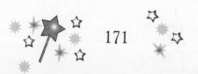

171

fear the time really has come," he said, "for us to return to Zavania."

"Isabella's brother Orlando will take you in one of my chariots," said Tatiana.

"That is very kind of you," Sebastian replied, "but if it is at all possible I would like us to stop at the gypsy encampment so that we can tell the gypsy folk they have nothing more to fear from the goblins."

"That will not be a problem," Tatiana replied.

As the friends were saying their goodbyes to Tatiana and Isabella and the other fairy folk, Isabella suddenly reached out and touched Maddie's arm. "Tell me," she said quietly so that none of the others could hear, "why do you wear that metal contraption on your teeth?"

"My teeth grew crooked," said Maddie sadly. "My dentist – that's a kind of tooth

doctor – says I have to wear the brace and that it could take a long time to straighten my teeth. I hate wearing it," she added, "because some of the girls at school, and one in particular, called Jessica Coatsworth, always pokes fun of me."

"Let me see the brace properly," said Isabella. As Maddie opened her mouth she reached out her hand and gently touched Maddie's teeth. "When will you see this tooth doctor again?" she asked.

"I have to go next week," Maddie replied.

"Well, I think he will be surprised to find that your teeth are quite straight now," said Isabella, "and that you'll no longer have to wear your brace."

"Oh," cried Maddie, "how wonderful. But how did you manage to do that? Sebastian can't use his magic in my world."

"Ah," said Isabella, "but I am a Tooth

173

Fairy, remember, and I'm always going into your world. Just you wait and see."

A few moments later they climbed into the beautiful golden chariot that was waiting in front of the main entrance. Driven by Orlando, it was drawn by two winged horses with coats as white as snow.

"Goodbye, everyone!" they cried.

"Goodbye," the fairy folk replied, "and thank you!"

As the horses flew up into the air drawing the chariot behind them, the friends waved until the palace and the townsfolk were out of sight. Then, with a little sigh, Maddie sank back against the luxurious padding inside of the chariot.

"Well," said Zak, "that's that, then." He chuckled.

"What is it, Zak?" asked Sebastian as he sat down beside Maddie.

"I was just thinking about the look on some of those goblins' faces as they were turned to stone," Zak chortled. "Still, serves 'em right, that's what I say." He paused and looked at Sebastian. "That was a good job you did there, old son."

"It wasn't only me," said Sebastian, "it was Maddie too. I'm not sure I could have done it without her – and you, of course, Zak," he added hastily.

"Just as long as you remember that," said Zak, puffing out his chest feathers.

It seemed that in almost no time at all they had travelled over the Enchanted Forest and found the gypsy encampment, landing gently on the edge of the clearing. Joel and Juliana were seated outside their caravan together with their two daughters, Luisa and Gabrielle, who looked as if they were completely recovered.

The family appeared delighted to see

the friends again, if a little awestruck at their means of transport.

"We came back to tell you," said Sebastian, "that the dreadful fate that had befallen the fairy folk was the same thing that had caused Luisa and Gabrielle's sickness."

"Whatever was it?" asked Juliana anxiously and all around them the gypsy folk edged closer to hear what Sebastian had to say.

"A spell had been put upon the girls," he replied.

"But who would have done such a thing?" asked Juliana with a frown.

"Goblins," said Sebastian simply, and at his words a gasp arose from the gathered gypsies and within seconds the dreaded word was on everyone's lips.

"They'd taken over the land of the fairies," Sebastian went on when silence fell again. "They'd kidnapped Tatiana the queen and were holding her to ransom,

177

forcing the fairy folk to work to earn the ransom money."

"Only it would never have been enough," Maddie added. "They kidnapped me as well," she went on, "but the others rescued both Tatiana and me. The goblins put a spell on Luisa and Gabrielle when they escaped – they would have overtaken you in time and forced you to work for them in return for the girls' recovery."

"So where are they now?" Nervously, Juliana glanced over her shoulder as if she expected the goblins to be lurking in the blackness of the forest just waiting for an opportunity to pounce.

"Turned to stone," said Zak with a squawk of glee. "Every last one of 'em."

"Turned to stone?" Joel frowned. "How did that happen?"

"Sebastian's magic," said Maddie proudly. "He used a spell to turn the

goblins to stone and free the fairy folk."

"But that's wonderful," cried Juliana. "I don't know what any of us would have done without your powers."

"We need to be on our way now," said Sebastian, "but we wanted you to know that you have nothing else to fear."

With the thanks and gratitude of the gypsies ringing in their ears, the friends carried on over the rest of the Enchanted Forest and into Zavania. Sebastian instructed Orlando to take his winged horses into the royal mews to rest and be fed before their return journey, then the three friends made their way to the East Tower.

Thirza met them on the steps. "Oh," she cried, "you're back. What sort of assignment was it?"

"Interesting," said Zak.

"Zenith hasn't returned yet," said Thirza. "Are you going to come inside and wait for him?"

"I think," said Maddie, "if you don't mind, I really should be getting home. I'm sure, Sebastian, that Zenith will be really proud of you when you give your account of the assignment, so you've nothing to fear there."

"All right." Sebastian nodded. "In that case, Maddie, we'll take you home."

It was nearly dark by the time they slipped Sebastian's boat from its mooring and slid silently away up the river and out of Zavania, and Maddie was grateful for the chance to settle down amongst the cushions in the bottom of the boat. She closed her eyes, while Zak perched in his usual spot at the front and Sebastian manned the boat.

"Maddie, Maddie."

Maddie opened her eyes and found Sebastian gently shaking her arm. "You're home," he said.

She looked around, for one moment unable to think where she was, then she realized that the boat had slid under the willows at the bottom of her garden. It was still dark, the only light coming from the moon and the lantern at the front of the boat.

"It's time to say goodbye again, Maddie," said Sebastian and his voice sounded quite husky.

"I hope you two aren't going to go all soppy on me," snorted Zak.

"Of course we aren't," said Maddie. She spoke firmly, but inside she felt a huge wave of sadness that was threatening to overwhelm her. Sebastian leapt from the boat on to the bank, then helped Maddie to alight.

"You will come back for me again, won't you?" she said anxiously as he took her hands.

"Of course we will," he said. "We can't

181

manage without you, Maddie. Just as soon as someone else makes a wish, we'll be back, won't we, Zak?"

"Yep," agreed the raven and even he now sounded a little choked.

"Goodbye, Maddie." Sebastian hugged her, then stepped back aboard the boat. Within seconds, it was sliding away through the willows and downstream.

"Goodbye, Sebastian, goodbye, Zak," Maddie whispered, but she doubted they even heard her, for all that was left were ripples on the moonlit water.

With a sigh, Maddie turned to go. Brushing away a tear that slid down her face, she made her way up the garden to the house. As she grew closer she realized it was frosty and that the grass sparkled in the moonlight and made a crunching noise beneath her trainers. Quietly, she let herself into the kitchen and locked the door behind her. All was silent in the house

and the night-light was still burning on the landing as Maddie tiptoed past her parents' bedroom door. She quickly undressed and snuggled down under her duvet. She knew from the other times that she had visited Zavania that in her world no time at all would have passed, and no one would know that she had been anywhere.

But she knew. She knew all about those wonderful friends of hers, Sebastian and Zak the raven, Thirza and Zenith, of the dangers they faced on each journey as they granted a wish and of all the new friends they made on each of those assignments.

She really hoped it wouldn't be too long before someone else made a wish, but before then she had her visit to her dentist to look forward to when, thanks to Isabella, he would discover that her teeth were now straight and that she no longer needed to wear the hated brace!

But maybe for now, if she closed her

183

eyes and went back to sleep, she might just be able to get back into the dream she had been dreaming when Zak had woken her ... the one where she was in Zavania...